UNCUT DIAMONDS

a selection of new writing

Edited by Maggie Hamand

The publishers gratefully
acknowledge support from
Arts Council England

Published in 2003 by
The Maia Press Limited
82 Forest Road
London E8 3BH
www.maiapress.com

ISBN 1 904559 03 4

A CIP catalogue record for this book is available
from the British Library

Printed and bound in Great Britain by Thanet Press

CONTENTS

FOREWORD

Over the last five years I have taught creative writing as a
Writer in Residence in Holloway Prison, at the Centerprise
literature development agency in Hackney, East London,
where the Write Out! project offered free workshops and
one-to-one sessions for writers on low incomes, at Morley
College Adult Education Institute and at many private
courses. During this time I have been greatly impressed by
the quality and originality of some of the work produced,
and frustrated that it was so difficult for most of these
authors to achieve publication. In addition, there are many
writers of different backgrounds living in the capital who
have so much to say, and yet struggle to find an outlet for
their writing. This collection of short stories and extracts
from novels in progress aims to reveal the hidden talent
of these writers, many of whom have not before had their
voices heard, and also to enable other readers to gain as
much pleasure from their writing as I have.

This collection would not have been possible without
the support of Dana Captainino of Collage Arts, Eva Lewin
at Centerprise, and from Arts Council England for a
generous grant towards the costs of production.

These are stunning stories. Enjoy them!

Maggie Hamand
London 2003

the races

NATHALIE ABI-EZZI

GERRY INSISTS. 'It'll be fun!'

We're standing in Leicester Square and a Chinese man has just finished engraving my name on a grain of rice. Now he hands it over to me in a little sky-blue box, and I give him the money. Gerry thinks it's silly, but we don't have such things back in Argentina.

'So what d'you say?'

'What?'

'The races. D'you wanna go?'

'I don't know. I'm tired. I've been queuing all morning.'

'Go on, Ursula, it'll cheer you up! Anyhow, I've somethin' to tell you later.' He squeezes my hand and his blue eyes are excited, as if it is a delicious secret that he simply knows is going to make me very happy. And suddenly I'm breathless because I think I already know what it is.

'I have something to tell you, too.'

He looks troubled. 'Not 'bout what you said earlier?'

I had told him as soon as we'd met that afternoon. I had buried my head in his shoulder and told him that I would have to leave, for sure this time.

'No,' I say, but he's too busy glaring at passers-by.

'So they're really not gonna let you stay?'

'I've tried my best. I went to the Public Caller Unit this morning, then to the Home Office again; I saw the same man I always get to see.'

'And?'

I see the man's face again: the way he pushed his glasses up his sweaty nose as he told me, and how they began to glide down again. 'There's nothing else I can show him. I've taken everything – my birth certificate, family papers, qualifications, everything. I thought it would be enough; that they would see how it is and give me citizenship.'

'But I still don't get it. What 'bout your family? How come they can stay here and you can't?'

We have never really discussed this. 'It's crazy. My grandfather, my mother's father, was British, so she has a British passport.'

'And your sisters? How 'bout them?'

'They changed the law. Any children born after 1981 can automatically get a passport from the mother now. But that doesn't apply to me. Twenty-eight is too old! Afterwards the Home Office told me I could have claimed a passport too, maybe; but of course back then in Buenos Aires we did not know that.'

'So they're just gonna split you up like that – a family? You and your dad back in South America, and the rest of you over here? That ain't right, is it?' He half laughs in disbelief. 'I mean, it's not as if you're like the rest of – ' He catches himself. 'You're a . . . a . . . what is it again?'

For a moment I'm hurt he doesn't remember, but perhaps the word has slipped his mind. 'A chiropractor.'

'Yeah, right. I mean, it ain't like you're not gonna find work or nothin' – you'll get a job easy. It ain't like you're gonna live off the system, is it?'

We catch the tube to Walthamstow and then a bus from the station to the dog track. We make our way towards the giant blue and pink neon-lit pyramid along with everybody else. This glowing monster must be as big as the Egyptian pyramids, and suddenly I feel as if I'm taking part in some ancient ritual from a faraway time and place. But slaves built the real ones, hacking and dragging thousands of stones in the unbearable desert sun. I can imagine them: endless rows of sweating workers, lined up in the African heat . . .

I had stood in line again all morning outside the immigration centre – what they call the Public Caller Unit – in the rain. Queuing was such an English thing to do, yet the line was made up of Indians, Japanese, Ethiopians, Canadians, all kinds of nationalities huddled beneath dripping umbrellas to form a giant multi-racial snake – a wet one. The old lady in front of me was holding a white umbrella, and it struck me suddenly that it looked like a great swollen belly, and I felt sick.

Inside, the woman behind the desk smiled sympathetically. 'I'm sorry, there's no possibility of extending your visa. Next!'

There's a crush of people outside the doors, and the words 'Walthamstow Stadium' flicker and buzz overhead in outsize letters.

Perhaps Gerry has been mulling things over these last weeks, and has finally made up his mind. It's a big step, getting married, of course it is, and we have barely known each other five months; but stranger things have happened.

All kinds of people are pouring inside now – not just the middle-aged men in brown caps that I expected, but old

ladies who creep along propped up by sticks, and young people too, the boys all got up in coloured shirts and Adidas
trainers, the girls in short skirts and glossy pink lipstick.
Then there are older women with their hair pinned up in
French twists or hanging down in curls, their partners in
dark suits and loud ties.

'Get your goody bags!' A boy and a girl are standing at
the foot of the escalators next to a mound of small white
plastic bags. 'Only 50p!' proclaims the girl, snatching up
two bags and holding them over her head like a pair of
chickens.

Gerry strides up. ''Ere you go, mate,' he says, flipping a
pound coin for the boy to catch. I watch as the boy fumbles
for change in his bum-bag.

*The last time I shopped in the local district market in
Buenos Aires, an old woman had greedily dropped the coins
I handed her into an apron pocket. A desperate look had
appeared in the eyes of the stall-owners that last year and
had intensified in the final few months before I left. Like
everyone else, they knew that things were bad; and perhaps
they were prepared for them to get even worse.*

*I left the country before things got too unbearable, just
over five months ago, and I watched it on the news or read
about it in the papers: how the economy had crashed, the
looting and misery that followed, and how people were trad-
ing items and abilities. It had come to that. A doctor might
offer his skills for a loaf of bread and a few tomatoes, a
grandmother might part with an heirloom so that a plumber
could fix her broken tap.*

*'Six months,' they had stamped on my visa. I was over-
joyed. Six whole months with my family in London! In that*

city where you could get lost and feel that you were almost anywhere on earth – anywhere except Argentina. And there was nothing left for me back home, except for my father.

'No,' he answered when I begged him to come. 'I never want to leave Argentina.'

'But . . . but don't you miss mother? After two years of only visiting – ?'

He clenched his jaw, and I noticed how grey his hair had become. 'Of course I miss her. Too much maybe. But I have to stay with my people, with my country. I cannot just run away.'

I was bursting to tell him that such feelings were stupid – not noble, just stupid – but I did not, because at the same time I was ashamed that my own ideals didn't stretch so far.

'And even if I wanted to leave, it would only be for a while, like you.' He turned away and recommenced measuring, weighing and pouring, as if his salves and pills and antibiotics could cure the economy that was rotting from the inside out.

I left him there in his pharmacy. I wanted to get out. And maybe it wouldn't be 'only for a while'. After all, in a civilised country they would see reason. They had to. So I sold everything – television, washing machine, curtains, even my bed – bought a ticket and left, expecting never to return.

Upstairs, the noise is deafening and the air is already filling up with cigarette smoke. The surroundings are stale and dingy. There are red seats and chipped plastic-topped tables for those lucky who are enough to get them, but only standing room for the rest.

We find an empty space, huddle up close together and start munching on the imitation Jaffa cakes and cheap chocolates from our goody bags. Towards the back of the room, hordes of people are gathering around the bar or fluttering around the betting booths like moths. In front, though, a sort of balcony looks down on to an expensive restaurant with waiters and tablecloths and upright, folded napkins; it must have a better view of the track too, and is already half full.

Here, television screens are dotted around, and suddenly flicker on to show close-ups of the empty, floodlit racetrack. Beyond and below them I catch a glimpse of the real thing every now and then, but it seems small and far away.

As the temperature rises and the first race draws near, a sense of excitement mounts. The noise begins to come thick and close like tangled blades of grass. Behind the voices and laughter, pop music is dimly playing from somewhere overhead. A small boy in red trousers darts into view. He shouts out a name but there is no answer. He half crouches, peers this way and that between the dozens of legs, then disappears again.

'Come on, let's grab some cards and place a few bets,' says Gerry.

He leads me through the crowd, and his eyes smile when he glances back to make sure that I am still attached to my hand. I feel sick now. The whole place smells of warm overcoats and deep-fried batter, and beneath that the aroma of perfume mixed with anti-perspirant. The brown carpet is sticky with the remains of countless spilled drinks, and my shoes crackle as they peel off it.

We stand in a corner scanning the names and odds in the first race. They are strange names. Many of them don't make sense to me: 'Close Escape', 'Cratloe Suppy', 'Win Little Girl', 'Lisdoonvarna', 'Staccato Affair', 'Miss Dish

Delish', 'Be Bopa Jubbly', 'Astute Pretender', 'Turnaround Gypsy' – but Gerry picks two and goes off to queue at the windows and place the bet.

I stay behind. This is not what I had envisaged. I wanted a quiet place where we could discuss things.

When Gerry comes back, he has a drink in each hand and a quarter of his pint has already disappeared. I am not thirsty, though.

On the nearest television screen, we watch as the dogs are put into their boxes. Almost immediately, a piece of fluff on a stick starts moving around an electric rail just ahead of them. Then a buzzer sounds, the fronts are lifted and the dogs shoot out. They are wearing coats with numbers on them, but to my eyes they look more like a group of gazelles with their springy run and thin back legs: fold, unfold, fold, unfold.

'Come on!'

'Go on, number two!'

There are a few cries, a little cheering, and then the sounds of disappointment.

I look at Gerry. 'Was that all the race?'

It was so short – not real, only a practice run. There wasn't even enough time to get excited. But Gerry nods.

Three races later, he has won twenty pounds and lost eleven, but I'm content because at least it shows that he's willing to take a risk.

'Look! Now you've gotta put somethin' on that one! If you don't, I will!' His thick finger has stopped halfway down the list of dogs running in the fifth race. 'D'you see that? "Ursula's Smile". It's a sign! He's bound to be a winner!' He turns and kisses me hard on the lips. 'Bound to be!'

Five minutes later he returns waving another betting slip.

I look around. 'Is there somewhere a bit quieter?'

'Don't look like it,' he says. 'Could try outside if you like. Get a bit of fresh air.'

I nod and we head to the far end of the room, down some stairs and out to the trackside. It's cold but still not entirely fresh; a haze of smoke shifts and moves through the spectators like mist. There are no seats, only several tiers sloping down towards the track, and we climb down to the bottom level, close to the dogs' boxes where it is less busy. As I put on my coat again and bury my chin deep into my scarf, I accidentally kick an empty beer bottle. It goes spinning and cackling into a corner, and as my eyes follow it I notice the private bookies on the trackside below us. They're calling out better odds and are surrounded by a group of quiet, more serious-looking gamblers – old men mostly.

'That's better, innit?' smiles Gerry.

I smile back.

The greyhounds are being led round the track by their owners – warming up like athletes, maybe – and a giant blackboard to the right of the stadium shows all their names followed by lists of numbers.

Gerry glances at his watch and then across to the track. 'They'll be startin' again any minute now.'

Sure enough, the dogs are packed into their stalls. The fluff begins its circuit, the buzzer sounds, and then they're off, bounding like snapped elastic. Leaping. Flying.

As soon as I arrived in London, I started chasing after a visa extension, and after citizenship too. I was staying in my mother's flat on the wrong side of Battersea Park. It was nowhere near as nice as my parents' house back in Rosario, but it was clean and neat, and she had made it into a home.

*And then there was Gerry. It had been an instant thing;
I had felt that squeeze in my stomach when I saw him. He
was with friends and smiled across the bar at me. At least, I
assumed he was smiling at me, but perhaps somebody had
told a joke and he'd just happened to look up.*

*My sisters turned to each other with that look they had –
a sly, knowing look.*

'So Ursula's got her eye on someone!'

'She's putting on her best smile!'

*It was easy for them to be flippant, though – they were
still young. Reta was twenty and Anni only seventeen.
Twenty-eight, on the other hand, was a completely different
matter. At twenty-eight I had gone through boyfriends like
socks, changing them with the mood and season. I reasoned
that at some point I was bound to come across someone
who suited me, and for whom I would also be perfect. Or at
least perfect enough. I had grown out of the idea that there
was only one person in the whole world for me, but I was
still romantic – romantic enough anyway to want to marry
for love.*

*So I put on my best smile, and Gerry and I talked and
danced and drank margheritas all evening. The salt stung
my lips but I didn't care. He was a good dancer and made
me feel as if I were good too. And there was something
down to earth about him that I liked. Maybe it was his
round, honest face, or his thick arms, or the rough, stubby
fingers with their layers of desensitised, dead skin, but anyway he was real. He wasn't going to dissolve and blow away
like the rest.*

*We saw each other regularly after that. We talked, and he
listened and nodded. And I knew from his eyes that he
understood, and felt safe.*

One thing we didn't talk about, though, was work. He was a builder – he installed kitchen units, built extensions, that kind of thing. And of course we didn't talk about the fact that all I had ever wanted, ever since I was a small child, was to be married and become a mother – to love and be loved. And I did love Gerry.

'Ursula's Smile' comes in second to last and Gerry swears.

'Oh well, never mind, eh? That's just the way it goes. I mean, it's not like anythin' serious or nothin'. Not like what's happenin' to you.' He shakes his head.

Some people are going back inside, maybe to place more bets or buy drinks, but we remain on the trackside.

'I still can't believe it. I can't believe they're gonna chuck you out! I mean, it ain't like you're gonna live off the system, is it?' he repeats. 'Not like them gypsies.'

'No,' I reply curtly.

I think of the gypsy women who walk up and down the Tube trains with their layers of bunched-up, flowery cotton, their headscarves and rotten teeth, their scribbled notices on bits of bent cardboard, and their silent babies strapped to their waists. The men come on occasionally too with accordions and tambourines, but it's mainly the women who are left to do the begging. Tube passengers look away, annoyed or uncomfortable, but few of them give anything.

'Anyway,' I say irritably, 'it all depends on whose eyes you're looking through.'

'Eh?' Gerry stares at me, nonplussed.

'People who don't have jobs, who live off charity, or "off the system". I'm sure Romany women would be shocked that mothers here go to work *without* their babies strapped to them.'

'Oh,' says Gerry. 'Right. Right.' But I'm surprised because he doesn't really seem to understand.

'But maybe even then they're luckier than some of the others,' I continue.

He rubs the back of his head. 'What others?'

'The ones who are lied to. They come here thinking they will have a good job and a good life, but they only end up being prostitutes.'

Gerry touches my cheek. 'What's the matter, Urs? What's wrong, eh?'

But I'm annoyed. 'Nothing. It's only that . . . ' I search around for the root of my anger. 'Well, British people are always complaining about the crowds, the traffic, the expensive houses, the price of beer' (this last one is Gerry's). 'And they complain because they don't know.'

'What don't we know?'

I sigh. 'Nothing. I just have a headache.'

Perhaps I will tell him one day. Perhaps I will tell him that people here don't know what it's like to work for next to nothing, all day long, all evening long, and still be poor. They don't know what it's like to pay sky-high taxes and realise that those taxes will never be spent on development or maintenance or medicine – that their hard-earned money will only disappear into some crooked politician's pocket. They don't know what it's like to step outside and feel afraid.

'D'you wanna go home?' he murmurs.

'No, it's all right. Let's stay until the end. Anyway,' I add, 'I wanted to talk to you about something.'

'Yeah, that's right. And I had somethin' to tell you too. Somethin' important.'

I wonder how he will say it. How he will choose his words. Someone near us is speaking Urdu or Hindi; then they switch back to English, quite naturally, quite easily. But this moment is so important! How will he say it? How will he ask me?

'You see, it's like this.'

It's not the right beginning, but Gerry takes my hand, then both hands. He looks me full in the face and his eyes are brimming. This is better.

'You see . . . you see, I've been made a partner.' He beams. 'Bill called yesterday. They've talked it over and decided to take me on. It'll be the three of us now.'

'The three of – ? Oh, oh, I see.' I barely have enough time to take it in, to smile and look pleased. 'That's wonderful, really wonderful.' I wait. There will be a follow-up, surely.

'It'll mean more work, maybe, but I ain't afraid of that. I'll have my name up there with theirs. And it'll be more money too – lots more money.'

I hold my smile and wait, but he doesn't have anything more to say. His eyes flick across to the track. The next race is up and he hasn't even placed a bet. I see the thought flowing through his brain, and a half shrug of the shoulders follows.

Behind my ribs, my heart withers. And that's when I realise that he doesn't *see*.

'We can marry next week. It'll cost you three grand.'

A friend of a friend of Anni's had said she knew a man who did that sort of thing. It was her who had put me in touch with Tony, and he was offering to marry me for three thousand pounds. The price had gone up since the last time I was in London: then it was only one thousand. A bargain.

'I'll call you back. I need to think.'

'As you like. I'll be here. You think about it and call me.'

I did think about it. It could be done – it wasn't so diffi-cult. But then there were the check-ups. Those people could turn up at any hour of the day or night to make sure we were together and that everything was 'normal'. And there would be questions, too.

I called Tony first thing the next morning. 'I've decided no. Thank you and sorry, but I don't want to.' I hung up.

I wanted to marry for love. Perhaps that was stupid – not noble, just stupid – but that's what I wanted. And I hoped Gerry would propose.

The race finishes and Gerry turns back to me.

'Didn't you say you'd somethin' to tell me too?'

I nod, but suddenly I don't want to tell him. This isn't the right time or place. I don't want to be out here in the cold, standing next to strangers, next to a dirt track. I don't want to be inside either.

'Well? What is it then?'

'I'll tell you later.'

But he pulls me back. 'No, go on. Tell me now.'

I try to turn away again, but he gives my arm an insistent little shake.

'All right.' I take a deep breath. 'I'm pregnant.'

Gerry's eyes grow large, large as fifty-pence coins, large as saucers, large as two full moons. He glances down at my stomach as if he should be able to see the bump there already, then looks back up. He searches my face intently for something, for some sign that what I've said is true – but apparently he doesn't find anything.

'Are you sure?'

'Sure? Yes, I'm sure.'

There is an empty silence, although around us the noise has not stopped.

'What you gonna do? I – I mean, about your passport?' he stutters.

'There's nothing I can do. They told me I have to go.'

He's quiet and chews his lip for a minute as if he's turning something over in his mind; and all the time he's staring at the feet of the person in front of us. I have noticed him too. He's a young man, one of a group of people who look like City workers, and he has dreadlocks.

Suddenly, quite suddenly, I want to touch this stranger. I want to *feel* the discrepancy in his appearance – the smooth navy blue cloth of his suit, and then those locks like lambs' tails. They would be a new texture, one my fingertips have never felt before.

Later, on our way back into town, Gerry proposes. At least he proposes that getting married is what we ought to do. Maybe.

The Tube train gives a great jolt, the brakes screech and we come to a halt at the next station.

'It'd mean you could have the baby here in England and we could carry on like before.'

I don't think, I just refuse. After all the wanting it, a stubborn voice speaks out and says, 'No. No, I'm not going to do that.' The obstinate, idealistic Ursula silences the hopeful, needy Ursula – strangles her right there – and Gerry and I part ways.

I walk back from Battersea Park station past the dogs' home. It's late, but there is barking coming from inside. Even though I've never liked dogs, it upsets me. I imagine them sitting in long lines of cages, being looked at daily, being examined and assessed and judged. Is this one good enough? Is it house-trained? Lead-trained? Well-behaved? Is it neutered? And perhaps most importantly, does it look right? Is it cute enough? Is it pure bred?

It's tough luck for those that don't make it; and always, that 'let-me-out-of-here' barking, as if they know – especially the losers. I walk by and wonder how many racing greyhounds end up here, and I think about how 'Ursula's Smile' came in second to last.

A few days later I lose the baby. I don't blame Gerry, though. Perhaps the little thing just didn't want to be born to such a man. Or to such a woman. Or maybe it didn't want to go back to Argentina, who knows?

After visiting hours are over and my mother and sisters have gone, I lie like a corpse in the hospital bed and everything is white: the starched linen, the staff uniforms, the floors, the walls, the ceiling. A nurse brings me a boiled egg, and I stare at the perfect white oval, smooth and secretive. I stare, and slowly, drop by drop, my hollow body fills up, stretches tight, then bursts. It splits open and pain leaks out.

Later, somewhere in the eternity of scalding tears and agony that has nothing to do with the body, a faraway, silent part of me gently alights on the thought that this was the right thing to happen.

The aeroplane circles once over London, passing through a blaze of evening sunshine and back out again. I gaze down from the window. Perhaps after all I didn't lose that night at the races. Perhaps I won. 'Miss Dish Delish'. 'Staccato Affair'. 'Turnaround Gypsy'. 'Astute Pretender'. 'Win Little Girl'. 'Close Escape'.

A hundred languages rise up and join the misty pall that hangs over the city, a blend of pollution and sunlight; and below, the city itself murmurs, swelling and throbbing in a million different voices. Amidst the grey, I can almost catch a glimpse of colourful materials that were meant for hotter climates.

Searching through my handbag a few minutes later, I come across a small sky-blue box.

Behind and below me, I have left my family: my mother and my sisters. They will be making their way, tearful and angry, back to the apartment now. And I have left my child – not quite a human, perhaps, but not a thing either. Tiny, but to me still an entire, whole, undeniable being.

Once, in Leicester Square, a Chinese man engraved my name on a grain of rice. Tiny, but I shall always have it.

lady of the dance

PAM AHLUWALIA

I DIDN'T REALLY enjoy the flat, even though I put so much energy into making it look exactly the way that I wanted it. I had to apply for grants where I could, or borrow – paying so hard through the nose that I should have expected a nosebleed. I was never satisfied though. I have spent so much time waiting for it all to turn out . . . for something, I don't know what, but something like happiness or content-ment to show up. Like a reward for all my patient suffering. Maybe this time, if I could just get the grant . . . change the windows and knock the kitchen-dining room into one. The next project was always the answer.

I'm washing up yesterday's dishes while dinner is on the go. Jerry's just come in. Smiling broadly, he wraps his arms round my waist and squeezes gently. Why should I respond? He's late, and it's me that has to get dinner ready, wash up, pay the bills. He's not even looking for work. I sweep past him to check on the cooking and turn down the heat, let-ting him know just how busy I am.

He must know that something is wrong. Bet he won't think it's got anything to do with him. His smile is abrasive. I know he wants me to smile back and then everything will be fine. And nothing will get dealt with, like why he let Jake miss gymnastics, or why his twenty minutes could run from one to three hours. In the beginning it didn't matter, I'd ignore it all as childish excitement or spontaneity. I didn't want to suffocate him or be the wet rag. I remember when he could pull a silly face or do a silly walk and I would laugh, holding on to the fact that he didn't mean any harm. We used to laugh a lot. Now I find myself holding my stomach, which is full of knots.

'What's wrong? Are you on, or something?' he says, trying to be helpful.

'No, my time of the month is not the answer to everything.'

'I didn't say it was. Listen, I know someone who can knock the walls down in the kitchen.'

I know I can't carry on being negative for much longer – not when he's trying so hard, but it's not that simple, is it? Otherwise how come I feel as if I'm climbing up my own ribcage most of the time? If I smile, I might as well write out a licence for him: please leave footprints here, here, here, all over me in fact.

'Who can knock our walls down?'

'Dave round the corner . . . he did his own roof.'

'I think I might get the home improvement grant that I applied for from the council.'

His eyes light up.

'How do you know?'

I look through the laundry to make up a wash-load.

'Can't you stop for a minute, I'm talking to you.'

I make an excuse but don't apologise, why should I?

He turns away, heading up the few steps of our split-level flat, into the front room.

'Mum!'

'I'm in the kitchen, what is it?'

'Come here. Quickly.'

I hear Jerry go to him, then Jake burst in, looking for a matchbox.

'What's it for?'

'The goldfish. Why did you flush him down the toilet?' But he didn't wait for an answer. He ran off with the empty box that I found for him from the back of the cupboard under the sink. I follow to see what's going on. Jerry's holding the dead fish between his fingers until the little coffin arrives.

'You were out with your dad and I didn't know what to do with it. Or when you'd be back. I didn't mean for you to see.' I hear myself try to explain.

It sounds pathetic.

'C'mon, your mum didn't mean to upset you. Leonardo wouldn't have felt anything once he's dead.'

'I'm sorry,' I add.

The two of them go down the cast-iron stairwell to bury the fish in the garden. I went to feed the fish this morning and noticed how dirty the water was. I almost changed it. I could have, but I said to Jake if he wanted fish that he'd have to clean their tank. I didn't mind helping. Anyway, I couldn't see the little ninja at first. Sometimes he would be hidden among the rocks and toys that peppered the open-mouth vase. My eyes roamed round the floating seaweed, where I avoided looking because I knew it was going to be bad. And it was . . . I scooped him out, an irrepressible orange striking out in a final stand against the green water. I didn't know what else to do and threw him down the toilet.

I leave the pot roast to simmer a bit longer and we all go up to the front room.

Jerry puts on the two side lamps. Jake and I plump the feather cushions that make up the body of the sofa. I thought it'd be really comfortable when I got the suite, and it is, for five minutes, then the thing sags like it's given up. Jerry sat down in front of the marble hearth to build a fire. It's something Jake and I like to watch. Reverently, he lays out the box of barbecue fuel, matches and sheets of newspaper. Then he places the pieces of white polystyrene blocks between the pieces of coal and lights it, holding the newspaper up to the fireplace like a screen. The flames begin to dance in shadows, telling stories of their evolution. Each flicker is a milestone in their history; hissing, spitting silhouettes curl and thrust their wild, supple limbs. Each flame twists and turns, keeping in its bosom a memory that finds no trace. Jerry sacrifices the sheet of black-and-white print which is swallowed up by the chimney mouth.

'There's a good film on,' he says.

I listen, half-interested.

'I'm going into work late tomorrow.'

'Oh, good. Does that mean you'll stay up and watch it with me?'

'Well, no. The grants officer's coming round first thing, to make a final assessment.'

And I know there's no point in asking you to see him, you won't be up till the sun is rising on the other side of the planet. This I don't say because I don't want an argument, not in front of Jake. Jerry doesn't care, if he's got something to say he'll say it, he doesn't think of the impact on anyone around him.

'It doesn't matter, you'd probably be asleep by the time the titles are over. Anyway, what's for dinner . . . when's it gonna be ready?' he says, stoking the fire.

Things continued in the same way for a couple more years. In the mean time I was made redundant and got pregnant again. I couldn't turn to Jerry. His answer to most problems was to go and slash their tyres. I went to the Citizens' Advice Bureau instead. They made a list of all my debtors and drafted a letter that I had to write and send to each of them. I gulped down breaths of air to drown the butterflies frantically flapping round my gut. They were meant to sort it all out for me, that's why I came. I couldn't wake up to a tide of letters from solicitors and credit companies any more. The sight of any more post gripped between the jaws of my letter box or the radar sound of the phone hounding me made me hot and breathless. I had to suck hard on the air to get any relief.

They said they had too many clients who couldn't write or hardly understood the language, so I would have to do it all myself. I hated screening my calls and hiding out. I wanted them to give me back my hall. They gave me a list of options. I hated the other clients and felt guilty, sorry for myself and angry all at the same time. I rubbed my hands over my face looking for inspiration, hoping that I was in some magician's escapology trick, and that any moment now I would be released. I left knowing that I could hand in the keys, get another job or let my bank repossess. The last choice was my only way out. I would never throw Jerry out or get the police in, and he'd never leave.

It wasn't long before Ben was born and the bank fore-closed on my mortgage. I had a few weeks to sort out emergency housing, storage, removal, people and boxes to help me pack. I organised it all silently, passing Jerry on the stairs without telling him. What was there left to say? Not that I kept any of it a secret, he could see the crates and

other signs. It was the only way. He could always take care of himself when he had to. And even land on his feet.

I float around from room to room packing some stuff, but mostly overseeing a small group: my sister and friends are wrapping and stacking like a well-oiled machine. I hear their muffled chatting and joking with each other. My pillows, sheets, cutlery and plates are organised into tea chests and crates. I'm surprisingly calm. There's a calmness, even as the kitchen units, fitted bedroom furniture and central heating are dismantled and the nuts and bolts neatly collected. Everyone does their jobs quietly.

My friends include Sadie, an old work friend who I happened to know indirectly through mutual acquaintances when I was at school, and Doreen, a neighbour whose child was in Jake's class. We were on the PTA together and had struck up a friendship mostly, or at least in the first instance, on account of these common interests. My sister Tara and her sister-in-law Sheena, who was a regular face at our family barbecues and kiddies' parties, also turned up to help. Doreen's husband came over to lend a hand with the loading and heavy work.

I did want to take the double glazing that I got with my grant – why shouldn't I? But it was too complicated to organise and I already had so many people to thank, so I didn't. I stand watching the empty hearth being pulled out like teeth, courtesy of a friend of a friend, on the promise of a drink. With the last vanload gone, I take one last look at my gutted flat and leave.

Not everything came with me. Most of it disappeared into council storage. I kept the children's stuff. I thought, at least if they have me and their favourite bits we could manage.

I scrub the single room that is to be our home. By night-time it's transformed with Jake's posters, paintings he did at school, Ben's mobiles and teddies, family photos and throws for our beds made from silk saris. We are supposed to be there for a maximum of six months. We stay nearly two years. I spend this time making up to the boys for being a single parent, losing our home, living like chickens. There's a long list. The trips and treats are their right, I convince myself, and nothing to do with guilt.

It's funny how the group or 'peak time' invitations, with my friends and their husbands, partners, families, stopped. Maybe it was a coincidence, and no one was getting together for dinner parties or bank holidays. We were all supposedly friends – bent each other's ears about our own, or work. We'd all be flitting and flirting round the room, with snippets of trivia to taste and sing to each other. Now I was fitted in – to elevenses and midweek lunches, as if I had suddenly developed fangs or some infectious disease. I accepted this new position. It wasn't really their fault – I suppose superstition kicks in when people don't know what happened or why. It wouldn't make sense to them, would it? And I didn't really tell anyone, just hinted . . . joked or moaned a little, at those dinner tables. Never really con-fided. I stopped taking it personally though, but the thought that I was no longer 'safe' or right to invite, that I might be prowling for a new mate, did bite me for a while. I could see in their eyes that since I was partnerless, I must also be needy and desperate. I flapped as hard as I could to stay out of that cage. It wasn't me. I was in no rush. I didn't need anyone else to think of or answer to.

Jake wants to go back to say goodbye to the flat. It never even occurred to me. I go back while he's at school to see if

I can get in, take him back after school – but they've changed the lock and the letter box is muzzled, which is satisfying. I don't know what to tell Jake. I go back to the hostel and phone Sadie; she suggests he writes a letter. I make myself a strong cup of tea in the communal kitchen and then make my way to Jake's school. He walks, scuffing the front of his new shoes by dragging his feet. He must have not had a good day. I pretend not to notice the shoes.

'Hi, darling, what's wrong?'

'Nothing,' he says in the kind of low, feeling-sorry-for-himself voice – you know the one – that people use when nothing goes the way they want.

'I don't know how to fix "nothings",' I joke.

He ignores me. Now's not the time to suggest writing a letter, so I wait for a better time. On the way to the car I tell him what Ben's been up to, I tell him we can get a takeaway but he ignores me. I tell him a couple of jokes and he rolls his eyes at me.

'Stop dragging your shoes, you're spoiling them,' I finally say, demanding a response.

'I don't care. You're late, why have you parked the car so far away?'

'There was nowhere else. I'm sorry.'

'Ade's mum was gonna take me to Quasar, but she couldn't wait.'

'Look, we can ask Ade to come with us and I'll take you at the weekend, all right?'

With this he was pacified.

I've had to fill in my address countless times over the last eight months, with no certainty that I'm going to be there for a reply. There's no privacy for any of us, which makes little difference because my head is permanently crowded anyway. Sadie came to see me at the hostel today and made me promise to go salsa dancing with her. I said yes, but I can't be bothered. I've got nothing to wear – I don't even know what they're wearing in the clubs and I'm sure I'll look out of place. I ring her from the pay phone in the lobby and give all my reasons which sounded fine to me as I'd rehearsed them, but she doesn't listen.

'You've got to stop hiding away and live your life.'

'I am.'

'When was the last time you went out, or got your leg over for that matter?'

We both laugh, but the following silence tells us where we can or should go from here.

'Come on. You need some fun, that's all I'm saying.'

The ground settles and I answer.

'I could always take a lesson from men.'

'What d'you mean?'

'Do what they do in times of drought and they're feeling horny.'

Not that I would, I have no urge, but I'm not gonna tell her that.

'They do that anyway . . .' she says triumphantly. 'Take a lesson from me, you definitely need to go out. I'll be round for you at nine.'

That evening I find myself queuing in a basement in Holborn for a salsa lesson, before the club opens.

'You mus' look in each uder's eyes,' Anna says in her low gutteral voice, '. . . and iss not a sexual thing. Okay!'

Don't give me that, who was it that said salsa dancing is like having vertical sex? What's with those hot-blooded Latinos – the women as much as the men! Their bums hanging out of their knickers and the tinsel on their tits, have you seen them at carnival time? Flaunting their round hips, slim hips, melon breasts, flat chests. Honey brown cinnamon skins or black like molasses, writhing in the streets, sticky, sweaty, sexy against the throbbing beat. Lusty, violent movements brazen in the sun. How many died last year? It must have been hundreds of them. All crimes of passion, please don't make me laugh.

'You forget about equality,' Anna says, stabbing her finger into the air and generously waving her hand. 'De man mus' lead, an' de woman mus' follow. Always. Is dhat clear?'

I feel uncomfortable, and allow a little nervous laugh to escape as Anna speaks to us. She asks for a female volunteer and demonstrates how the man gently squeezes the palm of the hand to signal a change of step, or how he will assert a little pressure to the back to signal something else. This code, which everyone in here knows, still seems very intimate if not sexual. Above all else, Anna reminds us to focus on the eyes.

She asks all those of us who haven't yet danced with a male partner to hold up our hands. Mine goes up reluctantly out of guilt and duty. There's someone standing behind me who quickly steps forward to oblige. He is about as tall as me, which I quite like, since it makes it easier for me to rest my hand on his shoulder. Any taller and my arms would ache. It's been such a long time since I went to the gym. My fitness level is zero. He's of medium build, with a tousled mop of blond hair and a dimple in his chin. He smiles confidently at me, with his keen grey-blue eyes. We're instructed to hold our partner by the thumbs, which immediately makes me feel unequal, like a young girl holding on to a grown-up. His hands are warm and clammy. I grow a little more nervous. I wasn't expecting to have to dance with anyone, I thought we'd simply stand in rows to learn our paces.

Anna shows us that our backs should be straight, and our bodies limber. Mine is stiff. I'm not used to someone formally leading, I feel very self-conscious. I tread on his toe but he doesn't say anything. He's quite relaxed and makes general conversation, while I try desperately to follow his lead, without stepping on his toes again, or going the wrong way.

'I can do the steps on my own, but this letting you lead, letting go, is very hard,' I say, trying to explain, without wanting to be personal.

'Isn't that the point?' he says, smiling.

I try not to think as I fumble to move in time with the rhythm.

'You must find it hard to trust!' he pushes knowingly.

If this is meant to be light banter, God knows what he's like with his friends. I don't want his psychoanalysis, so I joke.

'It's hard enough to be coordinated with the music, never mind you as well.'

I stare at the shadows on the wall facing me, or the coloured lights flashing, bouncing off the ceiling and floor. Occasionally I catch his eyes. I feel an awkwardness, like an irritation under my skin.

The pulsating rhythm and body heat at San Stefano Bar remind me of the fun I've missed over the last few years. Parties, clubs, saunas, the fringe. I don't imagine that any of these haunts still exist. They all have their moment. And this would have been fun in those days. Looking back at when I did that stuff seems as if it was only an old dream. The drum resonates in the pit of my stomach, moving up into my back and shoulders. I just want to forget about this man, whose name I haven't even bothered with. All I can do right now is cringe and pray to let the music possess me.

Jerry and I would share secret glances at each other across a gallery of faces, at a party, wine bar or club – re-assuring, confirming love and desire. He used to come and ask me to dance when the slow records came on. Of course we both knew the exact things to say. It was comfortable and safe. Chalk and cheese are what friends called us.

'Let's get it on' by Marvin Gaye was what he played to seduce me. My first time. I wanted his smell, the taste of him. His body was my home. And now dancing was just another thing I did on my own. I look at my dance partner for the night, we are standing real close, his warm breath blows softly on my hair; we just don't dance the same, he doesn't feel right. I can't help comparing. And there's no reason to. But that old cliché about time must be the all-essential ingredient that helps you get used to anything, even this.

I drive along the Strand, heading back from class. I take a left into Farringdon Road; a journey I know like the back of my hand. A route back with Jerry from this place or that, for my birthday or his. I didn't know how to drive then, even though he nagged me to . . . all so he could drink. His star sign is the goat and mine is the ram. It'll be my birth-day soon. Our horns clashed too long and too often. Where once it was a question of who made the first move and only a matter of an hour or two, it just got harder. Years of boundaries slowly eroding. Hours slipping into days and days slipping into silent weeks.

There are temporary lights at the junction of Clerken-well Road and Upper Street. A burst pipe has totally flooded the road and some men wearing yellow plastic helmets and ear plugs are digging up the road. As I wait for the lights to change, I notice the orange street lights floating in the water like goldfish. Dead fish in a dirty pond. I stare at them with growing sadness. Someone paps their horn and I oblige with a middle finger signal back, then slide into gear – slicing through the sleepy water.

The road home looks clear. I look ahead at the empty streets and feel hopeful again.

the angry tower

MICHAEL CHILOKOA

IT HAD BEEN a long hard day for Patricia Maberly. The day dragged long into the night, as the bus she rode suffered a continuous mauling from a snarl-up of traffic on the Kingsland Road, heading south towards the City.

Somewhere and time previous, the 'fat controllers' of the city had decided that today was the day to hold a tube strike and start an extensive programme of road works, which sent a plague of disruption on to the capital's streets.

She sighed heavily as yet another missed episode of 'Hollyoaks' ticked away around her wrist watch, adding to an already long list of woes. Disappointed, Patricia switched her attention ahead of her and the queue of seated bodies in front, to admire the cinematic view offered up by a tall dark building that stood head and shoulders above the skyline.

A tower of strength, the building mimicked the fearsome appearance of a huge sci-fi robot, an updated seventh wonder guarding the financial district from encroaching clouds of congestion. It stood deep in the heart of the city with a trio of lights beaming vindictive red, its rooftop lined with a predatory glare, giving the tower an angry exterior.

Patricia settled in her third row from the back seat perched nearest the aisle and watched the silent display of power with a growing sense of envy. How did it do that? she wondered. How come it's so easy for others and not me?

The building didn't answer, it just glared. Stood there defined, as if shaped by defiance. The tower emitted something, something that Patricia took to mean one simple message: 'Don't mess with me.'

Awed, she panned her eyes back along the corridor of street lights stretching from the horizon, back down the high street aboard the bus via the front windows, past the file of heads and attached earlobes, thus returning to stare aimlessly at her own personal space.

She'd had quite enough of gazing at something she couldn't capture, in fact she'd had enough of feeling intimidated by the tower's knowing glare. The red eyes now seemed to follow their admirer's trail and corner her on the top deck, to inspect this curious creature.

Patricia hated eye contact and she felt the tower could tell it was not looking at a kindred spirit, one who was at one with themselves, held firm belief in their foundations and feared no one. Instead it felt itself in the presence of a coward. Or so Patricia thought, as she wilted underneath the pressure. Timidly she looked away. It was clear now. She closed her eyes only to see dots of red stalking her in the darkness, the eyes speaking to her.

'I've been waiting for you,' it whispered. 'Well, come on then, explain yourself, tell me what exactly happened, and then once you're done just do me one favour, will you, tell me why?'

She opened her eyes grudgingly, seeing the distant figure of the tower glaring at her, awaiting an answer. A gust of shame swept over Patricia as she relived the day's earlier events. Why me? she thought, why always me?

'I've already told you which figures, Patricia, for God's sake catch up, will you.'

The boardroom was packed and Tim 'Saddam' Evans was going about his business in his usual proactive manner, hurriedly passing out handouts.

'Right, here's the figures for the McDermot account, five sheets in all. Take a look and see what you think, any questions don't hesitate to ask.'

Heads were down, folding and unfolding sheets, trying to make sense of figures which didn't add up. Patricia searched through, knowing something was not right, and she spotted it when she found page three printed out twice along with a number of other errors.

So did everyone else by the looks of things, all seeming to writhe awkwardly inside their collars. Usually when these matters arose it was up to Adrian Sherwood, Tim's main man, to say something, but he was off with flu. So, feeling safe in the knowledge she was right, with no room for error, Patricia stepped up to take Adrian's place.

'Excuse me, Tim, where's page four?'

'Oh, for fuck's sake, it's right in front of you, Patricia. just have a look!'

Silenced, she felt the pitter patter of tiny arguments kicking at her tummy trying desperately to get out, but she refused to let them run free. She was too frightened, but convinced herself she was above all that anyway and capitulated under the pressure of faulty good manners.

'Where's page four, what do you mean where's page four – it's right bloody here!' Tim searched through Patricia's handout, desperately trying to prove his point. He paced around the staff like a demented mob boss, growing more frantic with each revolution.

She sat there, caught up in a needle of self consciousness as the storm took off around her. She felt suffocated as the talking-to bared down on her, forcing her to shelter beneath her glasses. Briefly looking up for sympathy, Patricia caught the eyes of staff weathering the storm comfortably in their seats. A few smiles here and diverted eyes there let her know that a good time was being had by all.

'Erm, Tim, I think there has been a little mistake,' Linda, the next-in-line after Adrian, stepped out from underneath the woodwork to inform Tim of his little faux pas at the photocopier. Using her usual sympathetic manner that oozed all the silkiness of a coffee commercial, she managed to calm the situation.

'Oh, I see, Linda, ah ha, yes, that is correct, thanks very much for pointing that one out to me, Linds.'

'No problem, Tim, it's that bloody machine, we've got to ask for a different repair man, present one's just hopeless.'

'Absolutely, maybe you could look into that one, Patricia. Patricia, Patricia . . . Earth calling Patricia, are you with us?'

Thankfully she wasn't, but as she journeyed home she carried with her still the deep scars of inaction bandaged so tightly in her psyche that only the tower could see them.

And it stood there, as if still cross with Patricia, still waiting for an answer she was too ashamed to give.

The bus halted, but this time for a good reason. The bus stop's flag was raised starboard, the doors were flung open and the changeover of cattle commenced. Outside, sunk into the night, ribcages vibrated to the sound of pneumatic drills driven downwards by men with bad backs hanging on for dear life. The ground was broken up by sharp bits of banter chucked from man to man, lending the scene a chain-gang effect. As grey vapours sat smugly in the air, the smell of tarmac smudged the facial expressions of passers-by as they wandered through a maze of cones, vats and abandoned bulldozers cast out by the roadside.

Deadened by what she saw, Patricia peered up at the tower and imagined what life was like from its viewpoint. Did it ever just happen to glance down and pass judgements on what was taking place below? She cradled the idea in thought and reckoned so, and she felt she held a good idea of its opinions too.

It was hell down there, but the angry tower from time to time would occasionally look down and have a closer look. It would see all around its feet reeked corruption, brought on by standing in a square mile, for oh, so long. Every cluttered night, it tried in vain to gain a deeper understanding of what took place on the streets of fool's gold, only to get beaten back by the siege of headlights that assaulted this Kong of concrete. The slow-moving four-wheelers, taking their aim from junctions and alleyways with lit eyes, would force the tower to reel from the regular assault of light. Tonight was no different, and it with nowhere to go would race around the city, with its gaze screaming, eyes searching, for a target that symbolised all that was wrong with the crowded metropolis.

So when their eyes met in that vengeful bear hug, Patricia knew the tower was happy with its final destination. Rage and setting timed, combined with insecurities, forming the basis of an all-out attack.

The tower must vent its frustration, and her wounds felt every word.

'That's the problem with this city, no one ever says anything, that's why nothing ever gets done, nothing ever changes. But you'd know all about that, wouldn't you, Patricia, aye.'

Heads dropped and shoulders resigned as some of the disgruntled got off and walked. Patricia watched as in the distance their figures evaporated. She'd pondered their decision to walk as she remembered her own similar dilemma this lunchtime. Saddled over a VDU she frantically talked herself out of resigning her post, while sipping a Slimfast.

'I mean, he probably doesn't realise he's doing it, really. I mean, I'm probably being a bit too sensitive, I mean you've got to have a thick skin these days, don't ya, I mean it's not like he's said anything bad about my skin colour.'

'Oh, for fuck's sakes, Patricia, I said the Hopkins file not the Hopkirk. Oh, where's Adrian.'

'He's not in, Tim.'

'Oh, for fuck's sakes, could you sort this one out for me, Colin, muggins here has cocked it up. Again. Yeah, that's the one, the Hopkirk file.'

'Yeah, I mean, he doesn't mean it, it's just the stress, that's all, we all fly off the handle sometimes, don't we?'

'Gutless, chicken, spineless, you know all about that, don't you, aye, aye.' The disapproving glare jabbed at her wickedly, as the traffic stood still and soaked up more punishment from a mob of horns.

The tower continued to drive a cattle prod of criticism deep inside Patricia's wounds, forcing her to seek sanctuary behind the numbed heads in front. Another bus stop arrived and the cattle changeover grumbled on regardless, and soon a commotion could be heard. A stampede of voices growing as the bus driver shouted for passengers to move further back along the lower deck. The voices of youth chipped in to lend a hand.

'Yeah man, move, move out of the way.'

'Yeah, get a move on, blood.'

Jostled shouts continued as a third bossy voice could be heard breaking in, 'Excuse me, please, excuse me.' The stand-out voices, a mixture of bass and treble, crept closer, making their intent clear to all on the top deck. Soon footsteps could be heard on the greasy pock-marked steps as they raced for the summit.

'All right, easy, mate.'

'Well, hurry up then.'

'Nah, you wanna chill out, blood.'

'Well, get a move on then, both of youse.'

'Rah, hear this one.'

Eventually the voices appeared in the guise of mongooses peering out of the staircase, each searching for rich pickings. The treble-voiced youths were both boys, barely sixteen. One was Turkish, the other either West African or West Indian, Patricia just couldn't tell sometimes. The base voice standing just slightly below them belonged to a thirty-something executive type, to whom Patricia took an instant dislike.

The trio all saw the openings and converged on the empty seats near the back. The exec sat beside Patricia across the aisle one row in front, and the youths sat in front of him.

The bus carried on and the youths began to banter, while the exec unruffled his feathers by opening up an enormous broadsheet. Patricia darted curious glances at her new stable-mates, as they injected new life on to a dying bus.

The youths' banter was helpfully broadcast loud and clear on all frequencies so that people from all walks of life could catch the show.

'Bell her now!'

'Nah, low, that!'

'You're a fool!'

'I ain't gonna ring her now man, she'll probably think I'm a stalker or somethin.'

'You're a chief! I bet you're scared, you little pussy-hole.'

The young pair continued unabated until the cavalry of a mobile phone ring cut short their macho posturing, to the relief of all parents on board.

They raced like gunslingers to their pockets only to be outdone by the smooth assured movements of the exec who demolished his broadsheet into a neat Rubic cube of paper. Then pulled out his slick little willy and stuck it to his ear.

'Yes, all right there, Tom, how's it going? Yep, I'm going to the football match tomorrow, maybe catch a few beers, rice and peas, that sort of thing.'

His one-sided conversation was even louder than the youths' and drove Patricia barmy as the Gordon Gecko of the high street plotted his ascent.

'Oh, you're joking me, what? Well, that's Greg all over for you. The Arndale Project just can't be handled like that. I mean, he knows I can do the job, so that's why he feels threatened by me. Yes, exactly.'

The bus filled with melodrama, a pot-pourri of ambition that even curtailed the efforts of the youths into a low whisper.

Inside Patricia's head the tower's voice could predictably be heard digging up old wounds. 'Say something, go on, say something, he's being a nuisance, say something.' The tower nudged and picked, nudged and picked. 'Go on, he's a fucking nuisance, just say so.'

Why me? thought Patricia, why always me, can't someone else do it, but she looked around and all she could see was a bus full of London inhibitions, cattle dressed up as humans, who lay comatosed by worries that pulsated their temples with realities of a life's shattered illusion of waged security, too tired to fight, too caught up in a war. They could only manage to battle with their own consciences.

So, like all Londoners when entombed on a packed bus, she was alone.

'This city never changes,' the tower glared. 'You sit there pissed off about something and you never say anything just in case you disturb someone, boo-hoo. Peace and quiet – what peace, what quiet? Tell me, aye!'

Patricia's faulty manners continued to break down and the horns alongside Gecko raised their voices.

Inside, the bus continued the journey of stagnation that had taken hold since rush hour commenced. The climate was growing drowsy, BO was raising its furry armpits and as usual only the young carried the energy to complain.

'Rah, bwoy, it smells rank in here,' proclaimed the black youth.

'Yeah, it's well stuffy, too,' replied his comrade.

'Bwoy, yeah, get me, I can't be dealing with this nasal hostility any more.' And with that the black youth jumped out of his seat to open a window. The sliding slit of glass gasped for air, ventilating a dead zone. In a split second, though, the window was slammed shut by the executive's hand as he continued to babble on into his slick, tiny willy. The youths turned round fuming in their seats, and voiced their complaints.

'What's the matter with you man, it's stuffy in here.'

'Yeah friend, I can't breathe, you know.'

Baffled by their protests, the exec placed a hand over his mouthpiece and explained something down to them.

'Listen, there are other people on this bus besides your-

selves, stop playing about and making a nuisance of your-
selves.'

'Ah, shut up, you little *buppie*!' spat the black youth.

The exec, taken aback, roared with retaliation, 'Right,
you little shits, you think you can fuck with me, do you,
well you're wrong, ever since you've come on this bus
you've made a racket and talked foul language, now enough
is enough.'

'You what?' screamed the youths in unison.

Patricia held her breath as she listened intently, yet again
impressed by displays of defiance and self-confidence. Then
all of a sudden she watched as others tried to have a go.

'Yeah, you heard, that's enough.'

'Yeah, too right, I've had enough of kids like you
mouthing off as well, holding everyone else up, causing
delays.'

'Yes, come on, you've both had your fun.'

The youths slid back into their seats gobsmacked.
Amazed not by the exec, but by the gallery of voices offered
up by fellow passengers who they thought dead.

Patricia, however, wasn't surprised – she saw it for what
it was. A coffee commercial to smooth over the cracks, to
appease the senior member of the board, and a sly chance
for cattle to have a go at minor figures who offered an easier
target than that of a well-dressed official who paid their
wages or better still ran the transport system.

The stifled air regrouped and the Gecko got back to
business.

'Go on, now it's your turn,' the tower whispered as the
bus edged closer to its final destination. A sure sign of
progress, she felt pangs of guilt as the tower's face loomed
ever larger on the horizon, taking up more room in the front

window's display. The wounds were gushing again, raw as new.

There had been an error, she had seen it with her own eyes. The kids were loud but he was louder, it was obvious for all to see. And, yeah, it was bloody stuffy in here.

Just then Tim 'Saddam' Evans's despotic image flashed in Patricia's mind, ending all notions she had of making a scene and God forbid actually saying something to Mr Gecko. She was determined not to lose face again, so she opted for what seemed a safer option and turned to the smartly dressed female passenger sitting next to her.

'Excuse me, you wouldn't mind if I just opened this window, would you?'

'Yes, I bloody well would, thank you very much!' erupted the femme fatale. She was pissed off. Patricia had made the awful mistake of coming between her and her beloved fix of abyss she was currently getting from her opiate dealer of a bus window. After her eyes ceased glazing over the fatale's vocal cords offered a low growl, which signified end of conversation, and quickly returned to the abyss.

Patricia snapped her head back in front of her in shock reflex at the abrupt knock back. She trembled with embarrassment as she registered the 'nobody likes a do-gooder' reaction from the rest of the seated.

She was all right. She could handle it, just stress, that's all, it doesn't matter, we all fly off the handle sometimes.

Patricia looked for distraction and she found it across the aisle through the window opposite. Another bus stuck in traffic with a crumpled workforce on board. Another sea of faces all distressed and one in particular that appeared scared, too. A pathetic face that cried for mercy. Patricia giggled to herself, for once looking down on someone else.

What a state, she thought, poor cow. She scratched her nose and when she blinked so did her fellow passenger on the other side. And when she peered closer to see why they shared so much in common it finally occurred to her in a blink of an eye that the scared cow was her own reflection. Horrified, she turned away. A churning sensation appeared in the pit of her stomach and raced up her abdominal wall, tightening and relaxing as it surged along. It was somewhere in this moment that she decided to say something. As terrible as the sensation was it reassured her of one thing, she still had a backbone.

The Gecko meanwhile, unaware, continued to plot his ascent. 'Yep, I know, well Gavin doesn't understand strategy does he, he says he does, but he doesn't really.'

The air shrank as the suited one droned on. Patricia kept her eyes locked on him as she reached out simultaneously with her left arm to cross the femme fatale's path, in order to breathe more easily. Patricia grabbed the window slit by her neighbour, and slammed it open with an authority that sent shock waves.

Because this window was gonna stay open.

Noisy air flew in as the pneumatic drills celebrated Patricia's first triumph. Her neighbouring fatale was visibly shocked and tried to intimidate her rival by locking horns with tiny pin-hole eyes and bitchy growls. But she was face to face with a matador who this time wouldn't take her shit, leaving Patricia's opponent no option but to flee her rival's knowing glare by diving back into the abyss.

Meanwhile the Gecko continued to climb. 'Exactly, I know, I know, I know I told Gavin this but he won't listen. You see, I don't mind if people give me criticism as long as it's constructive.'

'I mind,' began Patricia. A simple bullet point shot from her mouth, somehow puncturing the Gecko's oxygen tank, leaving him gasping for air.

'Pardon, sorry, wait a minute Tom, someone here on the bus is trying to bother me. What was that you just said?'

'I said I mind,' Patricia repeated.

'Yes, mind what?' rattled Gecko.

'Well, if you just listen, you little shit, you might find out.' She paused to savour the moment, then she jumped. 'You think you can talk to me like I'm one of your trainee assistants, don't you. Well you can't.'

'What?'

'Ever since you got on this bus I've had to put up with your foul language and rude behaviour.'

'I beg your pardon.'

'Don't you realise there's other people on this bus, I don't care about your fucking business, and I don't want to listen to every minute detail of your personal fucking life, so I'm telling you once, and once only my friend, pack it in.'

The air hesitated.

'Tom I'll ring you back later, yeah everything's fine, don't worry about it, I just can't talk right now.'

The youths turned in their seats, slightly less fuming than before, to proclaim a glorious victory. 'See you ramped with a bad woman, blood, ha, ha.'

'Yeah mate, you little chief, have some respect for others, yeah.' They fell back in seats of laughter, taking deep into their lungs the newly arrived, fresh congestion charge of free air.

With that the bus itself breathed a sigh of relief and Patricia held her head high, proud to see her reflection. Energised, she pulled out her digital organiser and typed in a little reminder for herself: 'Must speak to Tim, clear up little matter re: photocopier.'

Happily she glanced up at the tower one last time to meet its glare. Its image seemed smaller, less frightening than before, as if knocked off a mighty pedestal.

Voices that had taunted were now silent. The eyes that had chased were now dimmed. Seated on her throne, Patricia had only one thing to say to that tower. It was a simple message. One that swallowed up the whole bus, making itself instantly clear, with its direct fearlessness.

'And you can fuck off an' all!'

the blue man

STEVE COOK

THEY TOLD HIM to take his clothes off and then they painted him blue. Stand on the plastic, they said, we don't want paint on the studio floor. One of them knelt down and began to work the colour into his leg. The other started on his shoulder. They used thick brushes as though they were going to slap up wallpaper paste and the blue was cobalt dark, thick like tar.

He'd thought it would be pale, lilac, the colour of his veins. They would tint him like a watercolour. As the curtain of blue was slapped down his back and crept slowly towards his buttocks, the smell rose, harsh and chemical. They wore masks, but they didn't offer him one. They didn't want to leave any marks. They were artists, or so they told him.

Stand still, they said. One coat, then, when it dries, another. Then we photograph you, then we pay you, then you can go home. There's a shower out the back. The studio smelled of clay and newly shaved wood and accomplishment.

I'm cold, he said.

The radiator's on, they said.

Why me? he said.

You're all we've got, they said. You were the only one

who answered our ad. Blue eyes, it had demanded, man with blue eyes. You weren't what we were looking for, they said, we wanted fleshiness, someone fat, perhaps vilely obese. You're far too thin. And then we thought, well bone, blue bone, it might work.

What is it you're trying to do? he said.

Just stay still, they said, and let us paint. We're the artists, you're just the model. They dabbled the blue between his toes, up his calves, over his hips, down his arms, around his neck, across his chest.

Won't I suffocate? he said. Won't my skin stop breathing?

You've been watching too many films, they said, bend over. He clutched his wet knees, his palms gluey, and felt the brush nuzzle him like a lover. Raise your arms. The brush licked along his underarm. Hold one foot up. Then the other. It kissed his soles, making him laugh, relaxing him. Enjoy it, they said, look at you – all bone and tense sinew, give in, your body's ours now. They combed the dark cream through his hair and taking a small, fine brush coloured his face with quick, delicate strokes. Don't smile now, they said, stand still and let it dry. He looked at the hair on his chest, now flattened but beginning to rise from its prison of paint. Thick drips fell from him, spattering the plastic. The hair on his arm had been converted into brush-strokes. His legs itched badly.

When it's tacky, they said, we'll put another coat on, then we photograph you. We want to catch all the drops and imperfections. We want to remove your identity, we want to make you the blue man.

He leaned his head forward, his neck cracking, feeling them tug at his cock.

We'll have to sort you out down there, they said. That's not blue, is it, there at the end? They laughed. Just a little dab will put you right.

He pulled himself away from their hands. You're not putting paint on it, he said, no matter what you pay me.

They went and had a chat as his hairs stiffened and the blue dribbled from his ear to his shoulder. The itching became insanity.

We could put a piece of tape over it and colour that, they said. Or we could use clay. Make you a little blue cap.

I'm off, he said, you told me this was art.

They put their hands up, patting the air around him to keep him on the plastic. Relax, relax, we'll leave it as it is.

He glanced back down again. It's so damned cold it's not like it makes any difference.

They had a sandwich and coffee from a flask. They put a second coat on while he was still sticky. When he was dry, he was solid. They had to teach their creation how to walk. They held his limbs and showed him how to bend them, how to stretch his arms, the rigid hair tugging away from the skin like teeth under his armour. Look at you, they said, you're amazing. Come over here, stand against the white screen, show us the contrast. He walked like an automaton, his lips pulled into a slot. Keep them closed, they said, don't let us see your teeth, we want one uniform naked shade, a man translated, a stark block of colour. They grabbed cameras and started shooting him.

Why blue? he said, startled by the clicks and the whirls.

They were eager to explain, gabbling like children. Think about it, it's the only colour that's cold, that suggests a thing without life. Any other colour has associations, of warmth and energy. You're alien, negative, a man without humanity. You couldn't be the green man or the black man or the yellow man. You have to be the blue man. Stand up, lie down, turn, crouch, kneel. They poked their cameras at him, shooting his outcrops of bone, his toes, the insides of his knees, the crude graze of his cheek, the tautness of his belly. The blue lay in puddles in the pits of his elbows, stuck in frozen bubbles on his legs, hung like caked lava in his pubic hair.

We've made you beautiful, they told him, you're our man.

Later he stands in the shower, ankled in a lake of blue, scrubbing at himself with a scrap of soap. The colour waterfalls off him, subsides to a trickle and then into drips. His old skin emerges from the chrysalis – rough, blotched and coarse. The blue man has been washed away.

I was famous once, he tells strangers – taxi-drivers, barbers, men drinking in bars. I was a model, I was the blue man. Oh, that was weird, they say, I saw that exhibition, they were creepy photos. I couldn't sleep for days. That was me, they painted me. Look, he says as he lies next to men in their beds, these were his fingers, this was his neck, don't you remember his eyes? That guy was a freak, they say, he was some kind of alien, no one knows what happened to that guy. No, he says, showing them his old worn skin, look, it was me. He clings to them, as they laugh and move their hands slowly over his body, I was somebody special once, I was the blue man.

the pink house

BELGIN DURMUSH

HARRY WAS AS CONFUSED as ever as he walked along the busy road. Once he thought he knew all the answers, but that was the time when his questions were an uncomplicated string of words peppering the simple, narrow path of his life. Now everything was a puzzle to him, and it seemed to him as if he was in a giant labyrinth, lost in its elaborate passage of confusion.

He blamed his parents. They were responsible for the chaotic frown that was his face. He even went as far as to think that they were there to drive him mad, not completely, like a gibbering idiot, but partly, enough for him to understand how mad he was, enough for him to see the glimmer of sanity waving provocatively at him from a distance. He thought he might be able to cope if their actions were meaningless, but their motives and aspirations were always clear to him, and for that he blamed them, for how could they show their madness to him so blatantly, and in such a way that he himself became a part of it? He wallowed in the icy clarity of their lunacy and took long walks in the filthy shopping streets, trying to lose himself in the frenzy of Life so that he might distinguish it from the frenzy of Madness.

He watched the speeding traffic with a serenity that he could not find anywhere else, and enjoyed his solitary moment in a crowd of jostling shoppers. But it wasn't long before a sudden surge of panic came over him as he heard his name called from behind. He did not dare look back for he knew that he would see the face of the stranger he knew so well.

'Harry,' he heard his name repeated. He turned back and cast an uneasy eye at the man who called him.

'Oh, no not you again,' said Harry, as the face he did not know looked pleasantly at him. 'I have told you before, I don't know who you are so leave me alone.'

'But I'm your father.'

'You don't look anything like him.'

'It's true, people change very quickly these days.'

'They get wrinkles and warts but they don't lose their face.'

'Your mother knows me. She used to know everybody until Spencer came along. Now she doesn't even know herself. She startles herself every time she looks in the mirror. She's bound to have forgotten who you are as well. I might have to introduce you . . .'

'We've already met, thank you,' said Harry sulkily, hurt at the suggestion that his own mother could have forgotten him.

'Then she'll tell you who I am. She knows me. She's never forgotten me,' insisted the stranger as he enthusiastically stroked his silver hair with one hand and brushed the bushy chin down with the other.

'I wouldn't rely on anything she says. She has her mad days you know,' said Harry, but then immediately regretted speaking so disrespectfully about his mother to a stranger.

'Yes, I know,' said the hairy man as the bushy hair shot up again. He tamed it with a steady hand and continued,

'Remember yesterday? The trouble I had persuading her that you were her son . . .'

'She almost wouldn't let me into the house,' said Harry, his tone dragged down by depression.

The hairy man laughed as if suddenly struck by a joke, 'What a mess! You don't recognise me, she doesn't recognise you. It's a good thing I'm here to remind everyone who we all are.' He stopped stroking his hair only so that he could smooth over the wild eyebrows which had jealously shot upright to attract the attention of a much-needed hand. 'Spencer! He robbed us of the little we had. How can I prove that I am who I am, Harry?'

The frown on Harry's forehead deepened and the expression on his face took on an almost mystical look. 'We'll have a look at the photo albums when we get home,' was his reply, as if somehow pictures in a book would set things right again.

'Would it help if I painted a beard over all my old photos, to help you see the similarity?'

'With or without the beard you are nothing like him,' said Harry, feeling that the hairy man was toying with him.

'I try to be.'

'That is not the same thing.'

'I'll practise at home to get it right!'

In a moment of unclouded clarity and insight which he would rather not have had, Harry felt that it was better to settle things in the familiarity of his home. So they walked side by side, like father and son, not speaking, which had a vague familiarity about it.

The sight of flamingo pink buildings soon dispelled any feelings of familiarity about Harry's home turf and brought him to a sudden stop as he turned the corner. The road, vibrantly pink, hummed with the voices of a vast crowd in the distance. Signs of wet paint were strewn everywhere, warning of potential smearing of clothes. Harry took a long step forward and left an imprint in the road which was lost in the mesh of footprints already making their way towards the Spencer house.

Harry followed the path that had been wrought for him. Each tread of his foot in the thick pink paint squelched, obliterating the calm hum of the distant crowd and bludgeoning the soft cumulous quality of the painted street. Harry was stunned by the unexpected gloss on every surface. He looked at the fine layer of paint and the willowy brush strokes caressed by the diffused light of the failing sun, and was mesmerised by the singularity of colour. It seemed to him that he was being transported into a land of dreams, so he plucked himself away from the fantasy world into which he was sinking and turned to the figure beside him. His suspicions settled on the head and beard when he saw thick pink paint that he had not noticed before glistening from the matt of hair. He dived into the mass of tangles and parted the strands, perhaps hoping to discover a paintbrush or a can of paint.

'What are you doing?' asked the hairy man, irritated by the ferocious fondling of his head.

'Are you responsible for all this?'

The hairy man paused, not wishing to implicate himself too early, and then admitted boastfully, 'I was bored. I painted the house but then it didn't match anybody else's so I painted theirs to match. And then I noticed something very odd . . .'

'Only then you noticed something very odd?' Harry interrupted.

'. . . The green hedges ruined the whole colour scheme. Do you have any idea how ugly the two are when you put them side by side? So I painted the hedges, and then the road looked so dull, and so I painted that too.'

'Didn't anyone try to stop you?' Harry asked as they followed the footsteps etched in the pink concrete.

'Nobody notices anything unless it lands on their head – but they did eventually. It's strange but their reaction was quite calm at first, as if they had discovered a land of dreams.'

Against his will, Harry nodded in complete understanding and dumbly stared at the turmoil unravelling around him. Cars splashed with pink paint lay on their sides like toppled turtles; fires blazed in bushes, and fierce, angry grey people clashed with their vibrant surroundings as they ran around screaming accusations at each other.

Harry ducked as a paint canister flew his way. 'You could have at least hidden the tins, now they're using them as weapons.'

'That's the fun of it, when was the last time you saw so many people communicating with each other so effectively?'

'Communicating? I thought they were trying to kill each other.'

'*That* is the ultimate form of communication; only when you are trying to kill someone do you have their full attention.'

Harry could not respond to this warped logic for it made perfect sense to him even when he didn't want it to. Another paint canister flew past him. 'I never thought people could be so unsettled standing in pink-blossomed streets. It's like trying to fight standing in a box of giant tissue paper.'

'Awesome isn't it? But Spencer ruins it a bit. I let him keep his drab colours.' The hairy face, still featureless and indistinguishable, suddenly glowed with animated pleasure. 'You should have seen it. Everybody was knocking at his door demanding to know why he wasn't pink, the same as everyone else. Poor Spencer even tried to paint his house pink just to get the people off his back. But it was far too late by the time he thought of it.'

'You really are a spiteful old man!'

'That'll teach him. I haven't got a face to speak of and he's to blame for that. No one knows me, not even you. It's no fun . . . You try having a conversation without a face. I constantly have to fight to be noticed.'

'By painting the neighbourhood pink and starting a riot?'

A flying brick fell at Harry's feet as another one narrowly missed his ear. The perpetrator, who was clothed in a crisp dark suit, mumbled incoherently and prowled along the road swinging his briefcase as he searched for more missiles to throw.

'We're not safe here, we'd better get into the house,' Harry said, cowering by the gate. He opened it and looked for something familiar but, as it was immersed in baby pink, he was not able to distinguish between his home and the pink house next to it. He knocked on the unfamiliar door nervously and his mother answered. Her tongue, which was covered in postage stamps, flopped out and wagged at him as he smiled at her.

'Yes?' she asked carefully, so as not to disturb the stamps which would have flown off her tongue at the slightest opportunity.

'She doesn't know us. Maggie, look, it's us, Tom and Harry.'

'Here we go again,' said Harry, his head dropping with disappointment.

'Don't be silly Tom, that's not Harry,' she said peering at him suspiciously.

'Mum, it is me, but who is he?' asked Harry.

'Who are you?' she said, wondering who 'me' was.

'That's your son, dear.'

'It can't be!'

'It is me, Mother. Please tell me who *he* is?' Harry asked again. She ignored him and popped her head out of the door. The sudden confrontation with the pink streets and matching buildings left her weak and disorientated. She wavered slightly. 'Where are we?' she said, the stamps fluttering in her mouth like golden butterflies.

'It's nothing, it's just a bit pinker than usual. Let me in, Mother, the riot's out of control.'

'A riot? I didn't know we had a riot, why didn't anybody tell me before?' she said, gleaming with pleasure.

'We thought you'd have noticed,' said Harry, as he watched the mob who were trying to break down the door of the brown house with a pink wheely-bin. No longer able to participate in small talk with his mother Harry tried to charge past her, but she caught his head and held on to it.

'Hang on a minute, who are you?' she said, holding the head tightly.

'Trust me, Maggie, you know him, you just don't know you do.'

'I do?' she said, slapping Harry on the head.

Harry held his head to protect himself from his mother, for he no longer considered the mob of rioters as a serious threat.

'I need to sit down. I'm beginning to lose myself.'

'You see, he doesn't even know who he is,' Maggie screamed, horrified at the stranger at her doorstep.

'He's just a bit confused, dear.'

'Well, this is not a home for the confused. What hope do we have if he doesn't know himself?'

'None whatsoever,' said Harry in what was becoming his normal dejected tone.

Maggie looked suspiciously at Harry, for there was nothing about him that she could recognise.

'I'll let you in, but only if you're sure that you are who you say you are.'

Harry nodded and entered the house like a humble visitor grateful for the invitation.

'Who is that man, Mother?' Harry said eventually.

'What do you mean, Charlie?' flapped the tongue of postage stamps like clothes on a line.

'My name is Harry, Mother,' said Harry, wondering if the conversation they had just had was a dream. He stepped closer, pointed an accusing finger at the hairy man across the table and whispered into his mother's ear.

'Don't talk about your father as if he wasn't here,' Maggie responded, 'You know how sensitive he is.'

'I don't know him at all. I've never seen him before!'

'Neither have I but he is still your father after all, so sit and be nice.' Her tongue wagged again as she spoke and a stray stamp veered itself on to a letter on the table. She thumped it into place and proceeded to the next letter, liberating her tongue from the stamps one at a time.

Harry grimaced as if an internal wound had suddenly flared up. He stared in disbelief, 'You just said he was my father – how do you know if you've never seen him before?'

'He told me when I opened the door.'

'He told you? But you've never seen him before. Would you believe me if I told you I was a cocker spaniel?'

'Oh yes, you always were a little tearaway.'

'Don't confuse her, Harry, or she might start patting you on the head.'

'Do I look like a dog?' he asked desperately, his tongue half hanging out with anticipation.

His mother looked at him and imagined his big ears as floppy things slapped across his face. But she soon dismissed the image from her mind. After all, he was not really hairy enough to be a dog.

'No, dear,' she answered at last, 'but you don't look like Harry either, but you seem quite certain that you are, so I won't upset you by contradicting you.'

'You mean you would let in anyone claiming to be me?'

'Only if they were convinced of it!' she said with emphasis.

'So I could walk in here tomorrow and find a million Harrys sitting at the table.'

'Don't be silly, dear, I would first check that I hadn't let you in already.'

Harry held his head again. This time it was not spinning, it just appeared not to be there. He touched it to confirm that it was still in its correct place then rested it in his hands. He looked at his mother who had now arranged the envelopes in a neat line and was peeling onions over them. He mumbled to himself, 'He could be anyone!'

'What, dear?'

'He could be anyone,' repeated Harry, pointing at the figure who was grinning inanely at some photographs.

'Not just anyone,' said Maggie, 'He claims to be your father, Tom. Why would anyone in their right mind say it if it wasn't true?'

Harry could not answer. The effort was too great for him. He walked over to the mantelpiece, exhaustion emanating from him as chaos ruled his head. A small mirror over the mantelpiece reflected a snug, quiet living room bathed in a hazy light, which gave the false image that all was normal. He stared at the mirror, bringing his nose closer to the glass in an effort to magnify the features in all their explicit detail.

'Mother, has my nose always been this long?'

'No, it never was. It's always been a cute stub of a thing.'

'I don't remember that,' Harry said as he pressed the flesh down to a bulging, flabby, blob.

'Don't worry about it, it'll grow back again when you remember who you are,' Tom offered helpfully, interrupting his perusal of the photo album.

Maggie looked worried, 'I thought you said he was Harry . . . I wouldn't have let him in otherwise. If the real Harry comes home now he'll be most upset to find an impostor staring into his mirror.'

Harry considered the likelihood of this happening. 'If he comes in, I'll hide,' he said, desperately.

Tom looked at his watch and abandoned the photo album to wait by the door, poised for the delivery of the newspaper. As if on cue, the evening paper flopped on to the doormat.

'There's bound to be something about this in the paper.'

'What? About us not knowing who we are?'

'No, not that . . . the riot I started. I could be a celebrity if I could be recognised.'

He opened the pages, searching for the article, and mumbled out the headlines as they grabbed his attention. '*Pretty in Pink* . . . no that's not it, *Pinky and Perky* . . . no

. . . *In the Pink*, ah here it is,' he said proudly, smacking his lips. He cleared his throat and stood up as if to indicate that the sermon was about to commence. Like an orator he stood poised, the newspaper stretched far in front of him, making it difficult for him to see what he was reading. Harry moved away from the mirror and sat down to listen.

Tom's voice carried itself boldly, ringing like a church bell as he read from the tabloid newspaper:

'In the unique blossom-pink neighbourhood of today's otherwise drab streets, a man was shot because he was a lousy painter, according to his neighbours.

'The neighbours, objecting to his colour scheme, shot him dead as he stood outside his pink house claiming his innocence.' Tom interrupted himself, dropping the priestly tone from his voice, 'He didn't have a pink house. I didn't paint his house. I hope they shot the right man.'

'He's got one now. There's a picture of him posing outside his pink house moments before being shot. Don't worry, dear; they got the right man.' Maggie said, dropping an onion peel on the picture of the pink house.

Tom continued, adopting his bold, formidable voice again for the task at hand. 'Proof of guilt was provided earlier this afternoon. A brown house, untouched by pink hands, stood unashamedly in the middle of a pink neighbourhood like a dirty speck in the purest of rose gardens. Spencer claimed that he was innocent but his beetroot blushing painted cheeks and his sad unpink premises were – as he was – a blemish to the surrounding perfection.

'Later that evening, rioters organised themselves in the best traditions of organised crime and formed a lynch mob. They soon realised that trees were scarce and since there was no possibility that he could be strung up from a bush, they borrowed a gun from a sixteen-year-old neighbour and shot him dead instead.

'Order has now been resumed and the neighbourhood is a quiet picture of pink health.'

'Oh! The riot's over? Nobody told me,' Maggie looked up from her onions sadly, the disappointment finding itself in her onion tears. 'The only exciting thing to happen and I miss it.'

Harry pulled himself out of his chair. It was as if a sudden weight had landed on top of him which was making it difficult for him to move with ease. He found an open album on the table and looked at it suspiciously. 'Have you been painting false beards all over Dad's photos?' he asked the hairy man accusingly.

'Yes, can you see a resemblance now?' he asked, hopefully.

'Oh, yes, that looks much more like you, Tom.'

'Mum, he's completely destroyed the photos.'

'I've just put a different face on things, Harry, calm down.'

'But it's not a real face.'

'Does it matter?'

'I thought it did,' said Harry, wondering if it did any more.

'Oh, no!' said Maggie, distressed.

'See, you've upset Mother with your false face on everything.'

'No, that's not it, I've run out of onions,' she said, alarmed by the fact that she had nothing left to peel.

'We'll go and borrow some from Spencer.'

'But he's dead!'

'So he won't mind then, will he? It's the least he could

do. I got his picture in the papers and he never even thanked me.'

'He's dead,' Harry pointed out.

'I gave him the spotlight. I gave him a voice and a face – ironic, isn't it, after all he did to us? If he saw himself now he would do a double-take.'

'Why, because he's dead?' said Harry.

'No, because he was a somebody at last.'

'A dead somebody,' said Harry, loaded by guilt.

Maggie interrupted, her voice strained by an anxious pitch, 'I'll start screaming if I don't find something to peel.'

All three stared at each other, then, as if by habit, each one picked up a pick-axe that had been on the floor.

Tom also armed himself with a shovel: 'In case they haven't buried him yet, he'll make good nutrition for the vegetables.'

Maggie nodded at the wisdom of these words while Harry shrunk imperceptibly.

All three, loaded with great big sacks, made their way to the back garden, towards the ladder that was propped there. Harry lagged behind Maggie. Maggie clasped Tom's shirt and Tom took small frightened steps into the dim light where enormous, bold, daunting shadows seemed to settle beside him like tenacious vultures in the night. Suddenly, the ladder appeared in front of his face and he was startled by the unexpected apparition. He stumbled back on Maggie's foot. She screamed and startled Harry out of his stupor.

'What? Is he alive?' he shouted, horrified at the thought of confronting a live person.

'I don't know why you're so nervous. Spencer wouldn't begrudge us a few onions. Not now he's dead anyway,' said

Tom, putting one foot on the stepladder and lifting himself over the fence.

'He must be turning in his grave!' Harry mused.

'If he isn't he soon will be,' Tom added, waving the shovel in his hand.

'They wouldn't leave a body in the garden, would they, he's probably tucked up in bed,' Maggie said calmly as she picked Spencer's vegetables out of the earth with frenzied speed.

'Remember that time he caught us climbing over the fence and he tried to knock us off the ladder, the inconsiderate bully,' Tom reminisced, climbing back over the fence towards home, laden with bags of vegetables.

Maggie nodded and said, 'I even tried to explain to him as I stood on this very ladder . . . there's never enough to peel at our place. I told him how I had peeled a loaf of bread once, and how the chicken was down to its skinny legs . . . but all he did was yell at me. That never stopped me though . . . all those lovely unpeeled vegetables, it was so tempting just to pop over the fence and fill up a sack every now and again. After all . . . what are neighbours for?'

They walked back into the kitchen where more onions and carrots were burbling garrulously in the pot.

'Don't upset yourself, Maggie. He's dead now.'

Maggie stood at the table and peeled. 'I can't help it. It's his fault that I don't know anybody any more. He poisoned me with his vegetables.'

'No, that can't be true – they're organic.' They stared at the vegetables in silence.

Maggie drew a deep breath, 'Eat your vegetables, Harry,' she said, putting a plate of carrots in front of him, 'After all, Spencer sacrificed his life for them.'

The light dimmed outside. Maggie peeled the tomatoes, the apples and then the potatoes and threw them all on to the mountainous mess on the table. Harry looked at the sacks filled with vegetables and thought of angry Spencer wielding a shovel at them. In spite of himself, he delved into the vegetables in front of him and wondered whether, given the correct sustenance, he too would one day become like his parents.

marta and jésica
go cleaning

ALIX EDWARDS

JÉSICA PRESSED THE BELL on the bus. 'Come on Marta! This is our stop.'

The street was wide. There was hardly any traffic. The houses were large and white with gravel driveways and front gardens filled with shrubs and evergreens. Marta shivered. It was cold, but for once the sun was shining and the sky was blue.

Jésica opened a wrought iron gate. They crossed a rhododendron-flanked path and walked up immaculately polished yellow ceramic steps to a post-box red door with a shiny brass letterbox. Jésica took her purse out of her handbag and pulled out a large set of keys on an enamel flower-patterned key ring.

'You have her keys?' Giving your house keys to a stranger! Marta could not believe such a thing.

'Of course I have them,' Jésica laughed, opening the door. 'That's *normal* here. *Gracias a Dios* she's never here to let me in!'

The house was warm, with oak floors and thick carpets.

'Want a coffee?' asked Jésica, as she hung their coats in a large cupboard under the stairs.

The kitchen was enormous with white wooden fitted units and modern contraptions plugged in everywhere. And in the middle was the largest cooker Marta had ever seen. A packet of real coffee and an Italian mocha coffee machine were laid out for them on a granite work surface.

'*Caramba!*' hissed Jésica as she picked up a sheet of flowery paper that had been carefully placed under a plate of chocolate biscuits. 'Washing machine, dryer, fridge, freezer,' Jésica pointed at more units behind her. 'Sometimes I put the washing on for her, but most days I just fill and empty the dishwasher.'

'Dishwasher!' exclaimed Marta. 'Not even Tío Eugenio had one of those.'

As Jésica showed her proudly around Marta felt she was in a sci-fi film. There was a machine for cutting vegetables. A machine for making cappuccino. A machine for toasting bread. A different machine for toasting sandwiches. An ice-cream maker, a yoghurt maker, a pasta maker, a bread maker. And one of those microwave ovens that Americans have.

'She must be very busy,' sighed Marta.

'Busy?' Jésica stared at her in surprise. 'No big deal! They *all* have this stuff . . . And look – ' she pointed behind her – 'these are all her books.'

Marta stared in amazement at row after row of cookery books, arranged by size, behind a glass cupboard. 'I bet she has some parties.'

'No. Not as often as some of them.' Jésica crossed herself. 'But she does like cooking strange things for her husband.'

Marta laughed.

'Come on!' cried Jésica before Marta could even finish her coffee or her chocolate biscuits. 'Stop daydreaming, Marta! Have you seen the size of this list?' Jésica waved Mrs

Richards' flowery notepaper under her face. But it was so warm and Marta was so comfortable, she couldn't face standing up. Anyway, what would *mamá* think if she could see *her*, Marta Cecilia, her youngest daughter, more than four thousand miles from home, reduced to this? Marta wanted to stay right where she was. Tell Jésica to forget it. After all, Marta wasn't a *campesino*. Marta wasn't stupid. Marta had an education!

Marta leaned her elbows on the table and forced her legs to push themselves up.

'Are you OK?' Jésica's voice came from inside a large cupboard.

Marta followed her. She was kneeling in front of a large green plastic carrier, filling it with multi-coloured powders, sprays and detergents. When the carrier was completely full, she put some J-cloths and dusters on top.

'You carry this for me, Marta. I'll get *el Hoover*.'

Marta tried to read the labels. *Flash. Domestos. Tesco's*, they said, but these words meant nothing to her. *El Hoover* was bright yellow, purple and clear plastic and small, not like the upright ones she'd seen on TV.

'You know something,' Jésica flicked the nozzle – 'these Hoovers are the best ones in the world!' Jésica tucked it under her arm and Marta followed her up endless flights of sage-green carpeted stairs.

At the top of the house were several bedrooms. They looked identical, with pine beds, flowery curtains and anemone pink carpet.

'These are the best rooms! Hardly ever dirty,' Jésica panted. 'Her children left home years ago and she only uses them when they come to visit or when she has guests.' Jésica sprayed a vile-smelling substance on the floor.

'What's that?'

'Carpet freshener. Makes the rooms smell nice when you Hoover them.' Jésica took one of the cloths from the top of the carrier and began dusting the windowsills. 'Give me a hand, Marta,' she said, throwing her an orange duster. 'This street soot,' she cried, shaking black grime on to the floor. It gets in everything here!'

Marta watched Jésica carefully and copied her. Marta had seen other people dusting, but she'd never had to do it herself. Dusting window sills for an Englishwoman! She was no better than Estéla, *mamá*'s maid.

There were china birds and Wedgwood vases on top of the pine chest of drawers. Jésica moved them all off, shook a brown hairspray bottle and squirted shaving foam on to the yellow wood. 'This is *Pledge*. When you spray it on the wood, it looks clean and shiny.' Jésica rubbed the creamy substance with a yellow cloth until it became invisible. Then she bent down to smell it. 'Are you sure you'll remember all this?'

Marta tried to pay attention, but each time her eye caught the window, she imagined herself sitting by the old church on the hill in San Antonio, with the whole valley stretching out in front of her, drinking Coca-Cola and eating sweetcorn and *empañadas*.

'Marta!' Jésica stared into Marta's eyes but they were blank. 'Marta! Are you going to help me or what?' She shook Marta by the shoulder.

'Oh! I was just –'

'I know what you can do. You can help me strip the beds.'

Marta watched Jésica, then reluctantly helped pull the sheets off the mattresses. They were all different colours. Pale pink. Sage green. If Estéla could see her now she would laugh. Marta had never straightened her bed in the morning, even when *mamá* had shouted at her, let alone made one from scratch for a strange Englishwoman!

'Remember each time you come here, you *must* change all the beds and make them properly. Then you take all the dirty sheets downstairs and put them in the washing basket in the utility room, or load them in the washing machine, depending what the note says. *Entiendes?*' Jésica looked at her seriously.

'But why?' The sheets Marta had just pulled off smelt of fabric conditioner. You could tell they hadn't been slept in.

Jésica pursed her lips. '*Así son los ingleses!!* They pay me good money. I do what they say. And remember next time, when you make the beds, be sure to pull the sheets down really tight like this.' Jésica did a karate chop and tucked the hem under really fast at right angles, as if she had been a maid all her life. 'That's the one thing Señora Richards likes to see . . . a well-made bed.'

Marta frowned.

'Your turn!' laughed Jésica as they went into the next room.

Marta threw a fresh sheet on the bed and tried to imitate what Jésica had done, but the ends looked creased and wouldn't go in properly.

'You fold them like this, silly!' laughed Jésica. Seconds later the sage-green sheet was tucked in like a hospital bed.

Marta watched her indifferently. What was the point in pretending to look interested in sheets and laundry and washing-up, even if Jésica was her friend? Surely she must realise that this was too boring to remember and, anyway, is wasn't her fault she couldn't get her head round it. Marta was just not cut out for this work.

'OK – now this is the difficult bit – the bathroom.' Jésica took bottle after bottle out of the carrier.

How unhygienic! Marta had never seen anything like it. The bathroom was painted all over, without any tiles except for three tiny rows above the bath and washbasin. The bath had lilac wooden panels. There was no bidet. The floor was made of wood boards, not marble. And, filthiest of all, was a straw basket with dead flower heads in it, placed on top of the toilet tank.

Jésica ran downstairs and came back with a new bucket full of even more potions.

'This is specially for the bath and the sink.' Jésica sprayed flecks of foam from a bottle that said *lemon disinfectant cleaner* but smelt like insecticide.

Marta coughed and ran towards the window, but it was locked.

'Oh. When you use this stuff, hold your breath,' Jésica said. Then she poured a gooey emerald substance from an orange plastic bottle straight on to the dirty brass taps. 'This is for limescale.'

'*Qué?*'

'It's very strong. Don't leave it on the taps longer than a minute. You just wash it off with plain water and then polish them.' Jésica splashed water on the green slime that fizzed like a sherbet fountain and buffed the taps with a white cloth.

Marta poured more green slime on the other taps.

'Are you crazy, Marta?' Jésica cried. 'Put these on!' Jésica handed her a pair of candy-floss pink rubber gloves. But they were way too small and stretched tightly over her hands so that she couldn't move her fingers properly.

Jésica pulled out a plastic bottle with a squashed neck and poured a thick yellow substance down the toilet, a smelly blue salt down the cistern, a green spray that smelt of vinegar on the mirror and sprayed foam in the bath. 'Got that?'

Marta's hands felt hot and sweaty. 'How will I ever remember all these things?'

'You'll be fine once you've done it a few times,' Jésica laughed, glancing at her watch. 'Come on! Let's do downstairs. Quick, before the *bruja* gets back.'

The living room was huge. The walls were an unwelcoming shade of blue. White shelves built into the recesses housed row after row of antique books. Ornaments cluttered every conceivable space. Jésica picked up two porcelain poodles from a corner unit and put them on the couch. 'It's the same as upstairs,' she smiled. 'Take these ornaments off and dust.' She pointed at a reproduction antique dresser. 'Only be careful with them. If you break anything, she'll fire you.' Jésica slashed her throat with her finger.

There were flowery plates. China birds, bigger than the ones upstairs, with drab-coloured feathers. And dull blue-brown statuettes of women wearing Victorian clothes, their dainty reflections glimmering in the brown wood. Marta lined the ornaments on the couch and dusted the dresser while Jésica polished the floor.

'That's perfect,' Jésica sighed. Marta looked down and saw their joint reflection in the table she'd been polishing. Their faces were indistinct. Jésica looked younger. Almost the same age as her. They hoovered the rugs and straightened cushions. When would they stop? Marta's back was beginning to ache.

'Just the kitchen. Then we're done,' Jésica smiled.

Thank God, thought Marta, looking at the clock. She could not believe it. They had been there less than three hours. But it seemed like the longest day in her life.

The door opened behind her. Marta screamed.

'*Cállate* – ' hissed Jésica. 'It's only Señora Richards.'

A tall thin woman, with snow-white skin and short grey-blonde hair, floated through the corridor, then mounted the staircase. 'Morning, Jésica,' she said in a cold, schoolteacher voice. She looked Marta up and down, but did not speak to her.

'Marta, wake up! *Despiértate!* You'll be late!' cried Jésica, shaking her shoulders.

Jésica drew back the curtains. The sky was grey. Marta pulled the duvet back over her head and rolled over.

'Marta, I'm going! I've got to go to work, now! Make sure you get up.'

'I will,' Marta promised.

'*Que te vaya con Dios!*'

Marta reached for the clock from under her pillow. It said 7.45. She jumped out of bed, grabbed a purple jumper, a pair of plain jeans and put on tang-blue eye-shadow and pink lipstick for luck.

'Are you crazy!' asked Jésica, buttoning up her coat. 'Take that make-up off . . . you'll give me a bad reputation!'

'But why? What do you mean?'

'Those Englishwomen. They don't like it if you wear make-up. They think you're trying to steal their husbands.'

Marta laughed. It was impossible to imagine that ugly pinched woman, with such a cold patronising voice, having feelings towards anything human, let alone a man.

Outside was freezing cold. There was no one at the bus stop. The road was choked with traffic. Marta checked her watch. 8.15 already. Jésica had told her to be downstairs by 8 a.m. at the latest. Marta hopped from one foot to the other, watching countless cars chug past. Five minutes, then ten, then twenty. Four 253s drove past on the other side of the road, but on Marta's side the bus lane was empty. Marta shook her wrist. What was the point in looking? It wouldn't make the bus come any faster. But as more cars drove past, she couldn't help herself. 8.35! What was she going to do? Then she saw the top deck getting bigger and redder in the distance.

Inside the bus was cold and filthy. The blue check upholstery was ingrained with the stale smoky smell of crushed cigarette stubs, in spite of the no smoking signs everywhere. Marta looked at the floor. It was etched with faint patches of unmovable vomit. They drove past the park under a railway bridge and turned into a bus station dominated by red and white hoardings advertising a football club with the same colours as *América*. Marta got off the bus as Jésica had instructed and stood opposite a shop selling football memorabilia. *Don't be late*. That's what Jésica had said. Whatever you do, *never* be late and always say 'yes'. Five past nine. Ten past nine. But the small hopper bus she'd been on with Jésica still didn't come. Marta checked the numbers on the side of the stop.

9.15, 9.20, said the clock next to the red Arsenal cannon. Marta tried not to cry. How right they had been to laugh at her coming to England. If she were in Cali she right now, Marta would be wearing her bikini, sitting on a sunlounger eating *cerviche* by the *deportivo* swimming pool, walking down *la 5ta* first thing in the morning to buy fresh *choclo* to eat on the way. Then Marta thought about the money: £4.50 an hour. How ashamed and disappointed Angel would be if she asked Tío Eugenio to lend her more and how, after all this time, could she even begin to explain to them why she hadn't yet enrolled in college?

Marta ran up the steps and rang the doorbell.

'Come inside,' said Mrs Richards, peering down at her through half-rim glasses. Her eyes were screwed up. She did not look pleased. 'You do have the keys? Jésica did give them to you, didn't she?' She raised her thinly plucked eyebrows.

'Yes,' said Marta.

'You do realise you start at 9 a.m. sharp?'

'Yes, yes!' Marta stared at the floor. What was the point in trying to explain how wrong it felt to use the keys to a stranger's house or that the bus hadn't shown up? Despite everything she'd learned at college, Marta couldn't remember the right words.

Mrs Richards showed Marta to the living room, where she took off her glasses and waved a flowery piece of paper under her nose, identical to the one Jésica had found under the biscuits. 'This is where I write what I expect you to do.' She put on a different pair of glasses and began reeling off a long, complicated list of cleaning and dusting and washing in pidgin English. Some of it sounded like what Marta had done on Tuesday with Jésica. But it was impossible to understand Mrs Richards properly because of her over-emphatic English. Mrs Richards sucked in her breath. 'Are you sure you un-der-stand?' she parroted.

Marta hesitated.

'*Com-pren-de?*' Mrs Richards replaced the small gold-rimmed glasses that hung round her neck on a glass bead chain.

Marta wanted to say no, to ask Mrs Richards to repeat what she'd said. But Jésica had warned her never to question the *bruja*'s instructions, so she nodded instead.

Half an hour later, Mrs Richards was still talking. Marta

tried to look interested, but all she could hear was the steady tick of the grandfather clock behind her.

'Do you understand? Are you sure you're listening?' Mrs Richards straightened her glasses.

'Yes,' said Marta. 'Yes. Yes. Yes,' the way Jésica had told her to.

'Any questions?' asked Mrs Richards when she had finished articulating something about washing and ornaments and plates.

But Marta could think of nothing, except how weird Mrs Richards looked, like a lizard mannequin, with folds of wrinkled net skin under the collar of her firmly starched Laura Ashley shirt.

'Maybe I'll have to ask Angél for money.'

'Maybe you won't!' cried Jésica as she stumbled in with the shopping the next morning.

'Tell me!'

'There's a job! Another one.'

'Cleaning offices?' Marta sat up eagerly.

'No, it's a house. Remember my friend, María Cristina?'

'Yes.' Marta did. 'The one in the pink mini-skirt who brought the cassette player to the party. The one from San Cristóbal who was here to find a rich English husband.'

'Well, she did it.'

'Did what?'

'She found a rich *inglés*. And guess what! She's staying with him right now, *fuera de Londres*, in a beautiful place called Essex. And he is so rich he has forbidden her to work!'

'Wow! Imagine landing a *novio* like that. But is he good-looking?'

'*Bonito?* He is stunning. Like a film star. And he is tall. And he is young,' Jésica giggled.

Then Marta remembered Mrs Richards with her endless flower-paper lists and pointless making of beds. 'This *trabajo* – what is it doing?'

Jésica shrugged her shoulders. 'Cleaning. And ironing. In a house.'

'Like Mrs Richards?' Marta's voice dropped.

'No! No! This señora, she's an old lady. She gives María Cristina things. She is very nice.'

Marta shrugged her shoulders.

'Her son, Martin, he's the *patrón*. The one who pays.'

'OK. I'll do it. But when can I clean shops like you?'

Jésica laughed. 'This is not Colombia. You need papers. And a National Insurance.'

'Insurance?'

'*Paciencia!* Marta, *paciencia*. Now is the wrong time to think about these things. You need to sign up for that English course first.'

The house was wide with a bay window like Mrs Richards', but there was no white paint or virginia creeper, just soot-black bricks, peeling window panes and three not five floors. Marta looked at the piece of paper. 78 Rochester Street. That was what it said. But how could that be? The garden was overgrown, full of crisp packets and tin-cans. The street was dirty, littered with paper and smashed glass.

San Antonio, help me. Marta walked up cracked concrete steps to a door with blue peeling paint and no doorbell. *Money is money. Money is money.* Marta repeated Jésica's words over and over again as she stood waiting nervously. No one was answering. There must be some mistake.

Relieved, Marta picked up her bag and turned to go, then the door opened. A pallid old lady with fresh marble skin stretched over her cheekbones, sparkly eyes and grey hair in pink rollers smiled at her.

'Come in, dear,' she motioned, with a crackly voice.

But as soon as Marta stepped in, she wanted to step out. Even though it was sunny outside the house felt cold and damp. And that smell! It was horrible. What could it be? Then Marta saw it: a big fat tortoise-shell cat, the size of a dog.

'Come here, Ophelia. Say hello to the lady.' The old woman bent slightly and clicked her fingers. They were long, fine and skeletal. And her hands were translucent, full of marbly blue vein patterns. Sit down, dear. I'll make us some tea. The lady ushered Marta towards a scratchy brown sofa. Marta sat down reluctantly. There was cat hair everywhere. Embedded in the couch. On the cushions. On the carpet.

'Want some sugar?' The old lady's wrist shook up and down as she dug a silver spoon into the porcelain sugar bowl.

'I think – ,' Marta started to excuse herself, then she remembered what Jésica had said. But Mrs Spencer didn't wave a flowery list under her nose and she spoke to Marta at the same pace she heard English people speak to each other on buses and in shops. 'I will miss María Cristina, you know. She's such a nice girl.' She explained to Marta what to do.

Good, no changing sheets every day, Marta thought.

'It's my arthritis, you see. I just can't get around the way I used to, can I, Ophelia?' The cat jumped on to her lap and purred.

Marta had three hours to clean the house and less than one bucket of magic potions. She decided to begin upstairs, like she did at Mrs Richards'. But the carpet was dark brown, with yellow flowers on it, not sage green or rose pink, and it was ingrained with cat hairs. The window-sills were covered in dust. The sheets on Mrs Spencer's bed were old and there was a lingering smell of sickness and urine. And there were no ornaments apart from some photo frames with a man in black-and-white and a colour photograph of a pale-skinned girl who looked a bit like Marta. Marta moved the window catch. She wanted to breathe some fresh air, even if she had to break the window to do it. Some paint flaked off. But the windows were stuck as if they'd been painted over. Marta wondered how long María Cristina had been gone. And how many people had turned up to take over from her and left?

Marta entered the bathroom. She looked under the sink for foam spray and tap cleaner but there was nothing there apart from a yellow bottle that said *Flash*. Unlike at Mrs Richards' house, this bathroom had tiles and a grey industrial floor, but there was no bidet or even a proper shower. The bath had thick white handles screwed into the wall and a white plastic shower curtain. Marta poured some *Flash* on to a scourer. The bath was filthy, not inside, as Marta had expected, but round the edge, which was embedded with black fur. Marta scrubbed the sealant. But the fur did not come off, so she went downstairs to fetch some bleach. It did the trick. Marta looked behind the shower curtain. There was more of it. On the ceiling and in between the cracked tiles. Marta poured more bleach straight on to the tiles. The fumes made her head swim. She tried to open the window. But it was stuck, too.

'But what *patrón*, what type of son can let his mother live like this?' Marta cried, as she sat down to rice and *tostones* with Jésica that night.

'It takes all types,' said Jésica, topping up Ramón's plate. 'Remember, it's not up to us to question these things. Money is money.'

Money is money. Money is money, Marta said as the bus drove from Mrs Richards' white house past a council estate to the litter-filled Victorian street of Mrs Spencer.

'Come in, dear,' said Mrs Spencer, Ophelia rubbing her back against her thick brown support tights.

The bedrooms were unchanged, apart from fresh cat-hair on the carpet. There was hardly any washing up or laundry to do. Marta wondered whether María Cristina had actually bothered to clean anything in all the time she had worked there.

'Today, I do the kitchen,' Marta smiled. But the minute Mrs Spencer went upstairs, Marta regretted it. The cupboard doors sloped downwards. The cooker was even older than *mamá*'s. And the kitchen units were made of wood that was sticky, brown and swollen where the ice blue paint had peeled off in patches. *Gracias a Dios!* Marta crossed herself when the first door she opened stayed on its hinges rather than coming off in her hands. Marta ran her finger along the cupboard shelf. It was lined with plastic-coated paper that had patterns of limes and oranges on it. The grease stuck to her skin like adhesive. Marta took all the rusty tins and sticky boxes out and piled them on to the kitchen table. Then she cleaned the cobwebs from the top cupboards and scrubbed them as hard as she could without ripping the paper. But it was as if they were coated with a strange brown varnish that would not come off.

Mrs Spencer handed her a green china plate and a large silver knife and fork. Marta tried to imagine that the bland potatoes were *tortilla*, that the steak and kidney pie was a palm-leaf wrapped *tamal* and that she sat on her patio back home, the sun glaring over the washing, drinking ice-cold mango juice, savouring the smell of fresh eggs and rice and yucca. Then Marta looked at Mrs Spencer chewing on tiny mouthfuls of food and felt sad. No one, not even the hardest person in the world, would condemn their mother to live alone like this in Colombia.

Marta turned the key in the shiny brass lock. The door sprung open.

'*Caramba*!' What was Mrs Richards doing here? Marta cried as she saw her familiar flowery back in the kitchen.

'Oh, good morning, Marta,' Mrs Richards sighed as if she was waving away a fly. 'Here's your list.' Mrs Richards retrieved the flower-print paper from underneath a box of home-made biscuits. 'Oh, and incidentally, Mr Richards is working from home today.' Mrs Richards peered down her half-moon glasses at Marta. 'You will bring Mr Richards his tea. One cup at 9.45 and another at 11. White with two sugars. Understand?'

'Yes, yes, Señora Richards.' Marta shuddered.

Although she had never met him, there was something about Mr Richards' sweat-stained socks and semen-soiled underwear that gave Marta the creeps. And now that he was in the house she wouldn't be able to put the TV on, or take her shoes off!

Marta poured the boiling water into a porcelain cup and plopped in two sugars and milk, just as Mrs Richards had said. She set some biscuits on a rose-patterned plate, put them both on a gold-edged tray and headed up the stairs. But the higher she got, the more difficult she found it to keep her balance. Damn it! She would have to get the money this week to buy some boots. These shoes of Jésica's, they were just too high!

'Come in, dear, come in,' said Mr Richards, a tall man in his fifties, with thin greying hair and a striped shirt.

Marta stumbled on the carpet strip.

'Put the tray over there – ,' he motioned at a leather desk with a laptop on it.

'Yes, yes.' The tea spilled into the saucer as Marta set it down.

'Oh, and do you think you can manage a smile? You *do* look glum.'

Marta wanted to answer back, say that she was no Estéla, but she checked herself. *Think of the money, think of the money*, she played Jésica's voice, over and over in her head. Marta smiled sweetly at him. Then she shut the door behind her, took her shoes off and ran downstairs.

Mrs Richards had left two huge piles of laundry and the sheets. The note said *wash and iron*. But how could Marta machine-wash let alone iron so many things when she was only there for four hours? Marta loaded Mrs Richards' pale pink underwear into the washing machine along with some of her shirts and looked at the list Jésica had made for her. 'L. *ropas delicadas*,' it said. They would wash the quickest. Then Marta went to the top of the house to strip the beds. Once she had pulled off the sheets, Marta walked slowly downstairs again, clutching the banister with one hand as she passed Mr Richards' study, trying to balance on her stilettos. So far so good. She threw the sheets into the utility room. But as she missed the kitchen step she went tumbling backwards.

Ow! Her elbow bone was bruised. Marta eased herself up, slowly rolling to one side then the other, so that she didn't have to lean on it. Then she saw the floor. There was a line of water coming from underneath the washing machine, like what happened to Tía Eugenia sometimes, when she said the soap container needed washing out. Marta got some dirty sheets and threw them on top. Please, San Antonio. Don't break down now. Wash these clothes for me this morning, Marta sighed as she made Mr Richards his second cup of tea.

'Everything all right? You look flushed,' sneered Mr Richards as Marta returned with the tray.

'Yes, yes, Mr Richards,' Marta mumbled, feeling her face turn crimson.

'And your arm. What's that nasty mark on it?'

'Nothing, er, Mr Richards. Fine. Everything fine.'

'Well, if you insist.' The corners of his mouth lifted into a plastic smile.

But when Marta got back to the kitchen, the trickle had turned into a puddle and she couldn't open the washing machine door. Marta threw more sheets on top of the wet floor. She turned the washing machine on. Then off. She checked the list that Jésica had made her and moved it to G – Drain: *desaguar*. But still nothing.

Dios mío! How can this happen? Marta shrieked. If only she could walk out. Get a plane home right now!

'What are you howling about?' Mr Richards strode into the kitchen.

Marta pointed at the washing machine. 'Get me out of here. I want to go home!' she wailed.

Mr Richards walked over to the washing machine and turned it off. 'I do wish you people would learn to speak English,' Mr Richards sighed, bemused, as he looked at the control panel. He raised his eyes to heaven, bent down and peered at the drum. 'Oh, it's that!' he snickered. 'The other one, she was always getting that wrong, too.' He turned the machine back on again and set it to F. 'That should do it.' He got up and took a packet of crisps out of the cupboard. 'F for Freddy. Understand?'

'Yes, yes. Thank you, Mr Richards.' Marta touched her crucifix. 'Thank you much.'

But suddenly Mr Richards was by her side. His arm squeezed her waist and before she knew it, he had pinched her on her buttock.

'What are you doing? Get off me!'

But before Marta could push him away, he'd slipped over to the fridge and taken out a bottle of German beer.

'Now, now! No need to get shirty. We won't tell Mrs Richards, will we, Marta,' he winked at her and sauntered upstairs.

the fry-up

NICK EDWARDS

JAKE LOOKED AHEAD through the thick, cloudy morning air and saw the outline of a thin white bridge approaching them.

'What the fuck is that bridge? We don't need a fucking bridge,' he said, turning to Dave. Dave's foot rested on the dashboard, his knee silhouetted against the lightening sky outside. His head hung down on his chest, his flat cap hung over his eyes.

'We don't need any money for a bridge?'

'I don't think so,' Dave said looking up sleepily.

'Where the fuck are we? There's no bridges between Bristol and Stroud,' Jake said, holding the steering wheel and looking around him at indiscriminate hedges and fields.

'We're in fucking Wales!' he said, turning to Dave and starting to smile. He watched a smile break across the brown skin of Dave's face.

They had parked in a service station just before the bridge. Dave, waiting for Jake to lock the car doors, was standing on one foot and then the other, rubbing his hands together. The cold air fell like smoke from his mouth.

Their two tall frames walked up to the wall that overlooked the river beneath the bridge. Dave pulled his jacket round him and Jake breathed in against the cold. Jake's longish hair fell around his face, he hunched his shoulders and pushed his hands into his pockets, looking down at his battered old jeans flapping over his trainers. Jake put his hands on it and felt the deep, cold, rough concrete on his palms. A white block of cloud completely covered the space between the water and everything above it. Fucking hell! How weird, he thought. He looked down at the water. Dull, grey and choppy, impenetrable, slapping against the shore like dirty swill.

As they walked back towards the service station entrance, Jake thought how uninspiring, nullified, dead this view was. This car park, the motorway, the city they had come from made him think this was all inevitable. But then, suddenly, he was glad they had ended up here because it was like a new, unexpected element to their adventure.

'Shit, it's like some desolate space station,' he said. 'It's quite surreal.'

'Did you see that weird cloud?'

'Uh . . .' Dave looked at the floor. 'My mind, quite surreal . . . Yes it is rather . . .' He waved his hand as if to say he couldn't actually think of any thought at all.

'Yes,' said Jake, looking at Dave's face, remembering he hadn't had any sleep for two days.

Jake's trainers felt as if they were slightly higher off the ground than normal. His feet seemed to walk extra quickly on this surface: his toe, then his sole, then his heel seemed to fly off the tarmac. He felt the gradual rising slope of the entrance through his feet. They entered the glass corridor and when they got to the entrance of the restaurant he was taken aback. The overwhelming burgundy colour of its interior, the bright lights and panels of purple felt on the walls and . . . everything. He stopped for a moment, Dave a couple of paces behind did the same. Because it was so early it was very quiet, this was when the staff chatted and stuff. The atmosphere was as if the place was theirs, not their customers'. Which seemed odd because it was a service station, which was for the public not the individual. Jake was suddenly conscious that they might be intruding. He felt like they would be told to fuck off if it was a second before they opened. But then he looked past this area to where the people sat down, and he saw a couple leant over a small table and someone else in the corner. They could be staff, he thought. No, they wouldn't be.

He walked in from the edges of the room to the centre. He felt conscious that the staff were watching him. He looked at the guy behind the counter, then looked again, jerking his head back. The man had an abnormally thin bald head sticking out of a starched white collar that left a gigantic gap of shadow around his equally thin neck.

'Hello,' he said and smiled at them very broadly.

The pallid white skin of the man's face broke into what seemed like hundreds and thousands of little creases. He was about forty or fifty. He wore a bow tie. Jake thought he might be gay. Jake nodded to him. He walked closer to him, he couldn't believe how the guy looked.

'Er, can we just get some food?' he said.

The man smiled and gestured with his hand to the hot food counter behind them where the dinner ladies were.

'Thank you.'

The man smiled again. Jake walked up to the glass counter. He looked at the sign on top of it: a piece of cardboard with a bright picture of a fry-up on it. What do you get? Three sausages, beans, one egg, a piece of bacon, some toast and a grilled tomato. £3.99 for that or £5.99 for that.

One extra sausage, one extra piece of bacon. Service stations are so fucking expensive! How much did I spend last night. £20, £40, £60, more . . .?

Fuck it. He pointed to the big one.

'I'll have that please.'

He looked around at Dave who was still standing by the door, at the back of the room, 'for no reason,' Jake thought. Jake could see his head hanging down, his hat shaking from side to side, looking up now and again and smiling to himself, his eyes looking watery and glazed, with his hands over his crotch. 'Why the fuck is he standing there?' Jake thought and walked over to him. The dinner ladies stood there, following him with their gaze. One looked at the other holding a big pair of metal tongs that rested on a tray of scrambled egg.

Jake reached Dave, and whispered in his ear: 'Don't you think this is like "The Shining"?' Dave looked at him. He was prepared for something but not this, his head fell backwards, his pelvis thrust forwards. He laughed out loud, exposing his sharp white teeth and the pink inside of his mouth against the soft brown skin of his face. He wiped his eye. The dinner lady, Jake thought. She was staring, expressionless, at him. He walked back over.

'Oh, sorry. Beans please.'

Jake picked up the tray. As he walked into the centre of the room, the thought, 'Why am I the one doing this?' arrested him. Where the fuck is Dave? What is he doing at the side of the room? He remembered how he'd always felt crippled by everything Dave had said or might think. 'Why the fuck did I feel like that?' he thought and remembered all the stuff he'd done before in his life . . . Whereas Dave, what's he done? Twenty-seven, no job, no career, lives with his mum. Hasn't even bothered applying for a job, let alone done one! Hasn't even gone anywhere, done anything. Shit, he thought. That's what happens if you don't do anything with your life. He pictured Dave standing in the blackness, the shadows, at the side of the room. He felt sorry for him as he continued towards the guy at the till.

Then, from behind him, at the counter he heard Dave's voice say: 'The same please.'

Jake stopped again. Dave didn't normally eat anything. He remembered in the warehouse he'd only eat a small cheese pasty all day. And now he's having a full fucking English breakfast! Fucking hell! He went back over to Dave who was leaning over looking into the glass, at the beans and mushrooms. Jake, with his tray, walked back over to him, leant over and whispered in his ear, 'Fifty pints, three hundred fags . . .' Dave's head turned slowly, looked around to see what Jake was saying, 'two scrambled eggs, two bits of bacon, four tomatoes, two Es . . . and nooo kip!'

Jake turned away. He didn't have time to catch Dave's reaction: his mind and laughter melted into one, like a long multiple division sum of the mind. Tall and upright, his mouth wide open, he pictured himself like a strange kind of dinosaur laughing in the service station. Shit, he thought, there's nothing they can do, as he carried on laughing. Then he straightened himself up. The dinner ladies stood looking at him.

He turned around still unable to stop laughing, and stood there for a minute, while his eyes watered, and eventually, through this haze, he realised he had to go and pay. He wondered what the guy at the till thought of him.

'Thank you,' Jake said.

'Thank you,' said the man in the bow tie.

Jake, holding his tray, strode into the seating area. As he looked around him, the sunlight seemed to be blistering out of the cracks of his eyes, he seemed to be radiating it. Picturing himself and Dave strutting through this service station together, he felt incredibly proud. Why am I feeling like this? he thought. All I did was buy a fry-up! Not the kind of thing to be getting really proud of, he thought and laughed to himself, and sat down.

Dave took off his hat and put it neatly at the side of the table. Bending his bald head forwards he rubbed his fingers over it, as if checking it was OK. The fluorescent lights made it glow slightly.

'I feel like we're trying to get away with something.'

Dave laughed and started shaking salt on his fry-up. His head seemed to roll on his neck as he giggled, then almost as if it was going out of control, he shook it to a halt. Smiling, his eyes watering and looking into the distance as if trying to focus his mind on something not his sight. Jake looked over his shoulder to see what Dave was looking at, reluctantly looking at this other world to see what was going on in it. A couple, fifty-ish, a women in a shit polyester shirt, black polyester skirt, sitting opposite a guy in a leather jacket. Jake was amazed at how typical of a service station these people were.

'My God, my mind seems somewhat fried,' said Dave. Pausing and looking at his food. He rubbed his eyes and looked down.

'Yeah, fucking hell,' Jake remembered again that Dave hadn't had any sleep for two days. He looked at the sponginess of the yellow scrambled egg. The pink rashers of bacon. Why did I buy that? He felt his stomach. 'God, that feels grim. Reminds me of that food last night.'

'Ugh.' Dave winced, and tuned his head away in disgust, his knife and fork stopped in the air just as he was about to tuck into his fry-up.

'God. That was so disgusting. Ugh.' Jake turned his head away as well. 'God, I was just stuffing myself, endlessly, darting from one bowl to another, not caring that other people were waiting and wanting to eat some, like a machine. Why did I eat all that? It was so pointless. You were sensible. You just had that one baguette.'

'Because there was nothing else to do.' He answered himself. 'We walked in. Absolutely pissed. And there's about eight people there. Sitting on sofas.'

'Yeah exactly.'

'Four or five women. All dogs. I had a bit of food. Nothing too grim.'

Dave laughed.

'And there was one gothic . . .'

'There was a gothic there, wasn't there.'

'Yeah, there was.'

'One really fat one who was just abhorrent, not even worth looking at at all, and then one who had glasses who looked like she was all right.'

'Obviously, the others weren't worth talking to, although I think I might have done, briefly. Christ, I sat by the one with glasses, chatted to her for a bit, she seemed quite nice, I think she was all right. But then I realised I was too pissed to actually pull her, and she was stone cold sober. So then I thought fuck it, and hit the buffet. I consciously thought I don't give a fuck what these people think, I'm just gonna stuff myself. I'm not going to pull so who gives a fuck.' Dave laughed.

'In fact in the whole of our night out in Bristol I saw one good-looking woman. In that first pub. The Hob Goblin.

You know the one, I pointed her out to you, she had tight jeans on and trainers and was kind of behind your shoulder, sitting in the corner, and she had kind of nice blonde hair. She wasn't like absolutely amazing, she just was you know just kind of chilled out. I thought she was just going to be like the first, and I thought shit it's going to be like this all night. Little did I know . . .'

'. . . that was going to be it.' Dave said looking him in the eye and laughed.

Jake looked down and shook his head.

'And that was in the pub which was exactly like the one in Stroud.'

'The place we were trying to escape.'

'Not even any, like, in all those clubs we went to.'

'No, there wasn't any.'

'Just a load of pricks,' said Dave.

'Yeah . . .'

'And what were those places like?'

'They were all pretty shit, come to think of it.'

'I thought Bristol was s'posed to be mellow . . . maybe we just went to the wrong places . . . and then the party . . .'

'Oh God, the party.'

'But didn't Doudsy say it was going to be packed?'

'Yup, he did.'

'That's why we left, and that there was going to be loads of fit birds there.'

'Yup.'

'Christ, there was almost no people there and some of the roughest women I've ever seen.'

'I think Doudsy has got some answering to do.'

'Didn't he say to get there early?'

'Yeah, he did.'

Jake leant across the table and grabbed the salt.

'And then I went to bed. For the next five hours.'

His eyes looking sideways, as if questioning his actions. I come to Bristol? I go to bed? he thought to himself.

'So what did you do?'

'Not a lot, my friend.'

Dave turned away and was looking across the room despondently, his eye gleaming with a ring of liquid around it.

'So who were you kickin' it with?'

Dave turned back with a start, as if surprised Jake was still asking the question.

'Just on my own,' Dave said.

'Wasn't there any girls there?'

'Nope. Just Tamara.'

'Tamara?'

'You know?'

'No.'

'You know, you know the one,' Dave said, leaning back, shaking his head, feigning agony. 'The tartish, slappery one . . .'

'What did she look like?'

'I dunno, just evil.'

'What was she wearing?'

'I dunno, some grim lacy thing.'

'. . . that showed off her tits.'

'That's the one.'

'Oh my God! I do remember her.' Jake leant over the table staring Dave intensely in the face.

'I know cos she looked at me like she was absolutely gagging for it, and so I looked back in a kind of debased way, you know? Pissed, and desperate for some action. And she looked back like, I dunno, like she was willing to succumb to my every whim. You know.'

Dave started laughing.

'Yeah.'

'But then, right, I see her turn to her boyfriend and I could tell, she fucking started telling her boyfriend how I was looking at her, in this completely depraved way. I could see her mouth saying it. So, God, then I had to like completely look away, so that it looked like I had nothing to do with it, so that there was no way she was going to get away with it. So it looked like she was talking total shit. And then when I looked back, you could tell she knew she'd fucked up. Fuck's sake.'

'God, that was it exactly.' Dave laughed.

'But what did you do?' Jake asked again.

'Ah, nothing.' Dave looked off again.

'Nothing!' Jake looked at him. 'For five hours! You must have done something?'

'Not really. Just sat on a fridge, drinking Red Stripe, and eatin' those baguettes.'

'I thought you only had one. How many did you have?'

'I dunno, I was just going and getting another one, all night basically.'

'But how many do you reckon?'

'Five . . . maybe eight?'

'Five, maybe eight!'

'Yeah.'

'Fucking hell. You must have had even more than me.' Jake pictured the amount of white dough in Dave's stomach. 'My God, that's disgusting,' he said and fell back in his chair laughing.

'Well I don't know exactly, but I just kept on going back.'

'Fucking hell, I'd thought I'd stuffed myself. Eight baguettes, three Es, twenty-five pints . . .' then there was a pause as Jake looked Dave in the eye, '. . . and n*ooo* kip!'

They both erupted into giggles.

'Work that out,' said Dave and put his cup of tea down on the table.

'But you must have done something for five hours? You can't have just sat on a fridge eating baguettes? Did you pull?'

'No, man.' Dave turned away and was looking across the room.

Sunlight flooded into the room and as the steam rose from their tea it made a beautiful transcendental mist all around them.

'So what did you do?'

As Jake stared at him a glitch occurred in his consciousness. He's still not answered the question. Have I done it again? It must be OK to ask now. We've been out together all night, we've only got us two for company, and it's just us two until we get back. Yeah.

Then he realised. They'd come far enough, he didn't care if Dave answered him or not any more. Fuck it if he doesn't, I've got other friends. It seemed much more significant now for Dave than it did for him. The steam from the tea twisted upwards through the sunlight, making beams fall on to Dave's face; as Jake looked down them, wondering if Dave was going to answer or not, it was as if he were witnessing the slow machinations of the universe.

Dave stopped eating for a second, his eyes looked upwards.

He is actually trying to think what happened, Jake thought. Fucking hell. I've transcended that level. Faith in what you're doing. That works. Everything's good now.

'Well, nothing really. I just stumbled around.'

'Oh, right,' Jake said reluctantly, expecting that this must be all there was to it. 'Wasn't there anyone else you could hang round with?'

'No, just Tamara . . . and the cockneys.'

'The cockneys?'

Dave's knife and fork stopped cutting the egg. His head swayed, minutely, to the side then he jerked it back. His eyes widened as he asked the question: 'You were there then, weren't you?'

'No, I don't think so.'

'Ah, you must have gone to bed.'

Dave stopped eating and pointed his fork at him.

'Luckily for you,' he said.

'What were they like?'

'Oh my God. You don't wanna know.'

'Why, what did they do?'

'Let's just say those guys were slightly perverse.'

Jake looked at him.

'They were just being this cockney scum, basically.' Dave threw his head back in disgust, holding his knife and fork upwards. 'Drinking loads of Stella and being incredibly grim.'

'Oh, right.' Jake nodded his head and turned away again. 'What where they wearing?' he asked.

'I dunno.'

'Ralph Lauren shirts?'

'Yeah, that kind of thing.'

'Oh right. Real scum,' Jake said.

'Yeah, just towny fucks. Scum basically.'

'What time did they arrive?'

'I dunno, about two.'

'What had they been doing?'

'I dunno. They just arrived, yeah? And they'd already been drinking for, I dunno, all day . . . and then they just started being this vile cockney scum basically . . . urgh. God,' he said, throwing his head back in disgust again.

'Man, that Tamara though.' The tone in Dave's voice made Jake look up.

'Oh God! That was it. That bloody Tamara. My God . . . Tamara, yes. Let's just say that was one dirty lady.'

'Why, what happened?'

'Ugh, ugh . . . Strange girl. She was just a dog.' Then he started humming to himself and looked away. Jake looked at Dave, slightly shocked. Dave carried on.

'My God. That was one dirty, dirty bitch.'

Shit, she can't have been that bad, Jake thought. He was surprised to hear these words come from Dave's mouth. I know I was just slagging her off but she doesn't deserve that. Some people would say misogynistic . . .

As Jake looked at him, it was as if a void hung between them across the table. He sat back in shock. Then he remembered, Dave wasn't like an old friend. I don't have to hang around with him again, if I don't want to . . . once we've got back to Stroud. He imagined the motorway home, it seemed clear. He felt relieved. But I hardly know him, he thought. It doesn't really matter what I think. I don't want to judge him. My friend. I don't even know what misogynism means, exactly.

He decided to try and change the conversation.

'Wasn't there anyone else up?'

'No. When they arrived everybody else thought fuck this and went to bed.'

'Oh, right,' said Jake looking at the table.

'I tell you what, I thought there was gonna be a gang rape.'

Jake looked up.

'Why, what happened?'

'I mean those guys were fucking vile bastards. But she was going along with it.'

'With what?'

'Oh, sorry.'

Dave put his knife and fork down.

'Well she was just . . . Oh God!' Dave threw his head back into the air again, '. . . there being her disgusting flirty self.' Jake gave up, and looked off into the cafeteria. 'I don't wanna think about it. It was just grim. Being a . . .'

'A strumpet,' Jake said laughing.

'Yeah, that's it.' Dave looked back at him. 'That's exactly the word for it. And because the cockneys were a bit pissed, they started getting the wrong idea.

'I tell you what, I thought there was gonna be a gang rape,' Dave said, looking him in the eye again.

'Fucking hell. What happened?'

'They were going . . .,' Steve put on an exaggerated sickly cockney accent, '"Come on, Tamara, you get yer tits out, we'll get our cocks out."'

'Is that what they were saying?'

'Yeah, man. That's what they were saying.'

'You're joking.'

'No, man. I'm serious. It was grim, man. I tell you.'

'What did she say?'

'She was bloody encouraging them.'

'Oh my God, you're joking? How? What was she doing?'

'Oh God! I don't know, anything that was grim, flirtatious . . . Just dirty, filthy . . . evil.'

'What like?'

'I don't know.' Dave leant back in the chair. 'Just saying stuff like "Oh, you boys, don't ravish me." I dunno, acting like a complete I don't know what. Kind of tittering, saying she would.'

'Get her tits out?'

'Yeah.' Dave laughed, seeing Jake's astonishment. 'Yeah. I tell you, man, it was grim.'

Jake paused, taken aback; he looked down at his scrambled egg, staring into it.

'That is grim.'

'I know, man,' said Dave laughing. 'It was so, so . . . evil. Is the only way to describe it.'

'It's almost worse of her to actually be into it,' Jake said. 'So low.' Then he looked up. 'So then what happened?'

'Then this one guy did.'

'You're kidding.'

'No. And then another gets his out.'

Dave looked at Jake as if to say he couldn't explain it, his head starting to shake with laughter.

'So what were you doing all this time?'

'I'm just sat there drinking this can. While all these guys are getting their cocks out,' Dave said bemusedly. It occurred to Jake how funny it was. He looked up at Dave, whose head was shaking and then his silver knife and fork chinked as he dropped them into the white porcelain plate, as he started laughing.

'What is she doing?'

'She was just tittering, going, "Ooh, isn't it squidgy?"'

Jake looked at Dave in disbelief. All he could see was Dave almost falling into his fry-up. His vision was restricted, as if he were looking out of a triangular void, the sides of it shimmering as if water was running over it. Like a protective sheen around them.

'What did they say?'

'They started going, "Come on, Tamara, we got our cocks out now you getcha tits out,"' Dave said loudly.

Jake became conscious again that people around them could hear, that they were laughing very loudly, especially at breakfast time in a service station.

'I'm sure these peeps is enjoying our conversation,' Jake said.

'Yes,' Dave said looking at them briefly and laughed again, holding his knife up. Jake tried to shut up. Not wanting to disrupt other people's peace but at the same time knowing it wouldn't threaten them if they did, so not stopping. He felt his shoulders cower in, trying to make themselves take up smaller space, and it made it more funny. Tears were in his eyes. Shimmering water over everything he could see out of this inverted void.

He looked at Dave holding the end of his knife in the plate as he stopped eating, to laugh. He realised they might get chucked out. Can we get chucked out? We haven't actually done anything. Can't be done for laughing, not that loudly, having a good time. You can't have a good time in this service station. I've only just this second stopped eating, so . . . fuck 'em.

'Did she get her tits out?'

'No, man, she wouldn't, she started acting like she was going to, but then it started getting nasty.'

Dave's eyes opened wide again.

'The cockneys started getting pissed off.'

'Yeah?'

'Well, then she realised she'd gone a little bit too far and that basically she couldn't handle it. And so,' Dave said, pointing his palm out across the table and looking outraged, 'she asks me if I'd be her boyfriend!'

'What?'

'Well, pretend to be. And I'm looking at her thinking why the fuck would I want to pretend to be your boyfriend?'

'And "No," basically.'

'Yeah exactly, No. So I said why? And she goes, "Because I'm scared of what those boys might do." So basically I had to sit there pretending to be her boyfriend, so that they didn't gang rape her! Which was nice for me,' he finished, looking like he'd just eaten something vile.

'Good you did it though,' Jake said.

He is a real person! Jake thought, looking at him. Here was this dole-ite bum, who didn't do anything, and here he was being the one who saved the day. All these guys probably had normal jobs. Bought clothes from the right shops, so they look right, giving money to the right companies, other people who make money so they don't get any shit. Like businessmen. What do they do? Yet they get all the benefits of society. And then here's this guy constantly getting shit from everyone, who lives his life in his own way, and he's the one who saves the day. So fucking typical.

'What was her boyfriend doing?'

'Her boyfriend?'

'Yeah, that guy who was staring at me.'

'Oh, yeah,' Dave laughed. 'That's a point, she had a boyfriend anyway!' Though exhausted some last laughter bellowed through them.

'Exactly. The lucky bastard going out with her. Where the fuck was he?'

'I dunno, probably upstairs asleep.'

'Probably that guy who we woke up.'

'Yeah.'

Jake looked out over the room they were in, he looked at the people sitting over their tables. He turned back to his table, looked at it, saw everything was empty. Remnants of ketchup on the plate. A bit of egg. A tiny bit of bacon. Then almost subconsciously he realised . . . Fuck, that means our right to stay isn't never-ending any more. Shit, we have to go. Oh my God! I'm not ready yet. Shit! I can't drive. Fucking hell. We're fucked. Shit. He looked around. What shall we do? I could get another cup of tea. Actually a cup of tea would be good, maybe coffee. Jake got up.

'Do you want a tea, or coffee?'

Dave grunted, nodded his head, and pulled a pound coin from his pocket and put it in Jake's outstretched hand.

'To be honest I'm not ready to go back yet.'

Dave laughed.

'Yeah, I can understand that. It's OK, man.'

As Jake got up he stopped for a second and looked into Dave's face. You're telling me it's OK. I'm driving you here. It doesn't matter a fuck what you think.

Then as he stared into Dave's face, he thought, actually, so what? And turned away to get the coffees.

As he sat down he said, 'Actually it's quite good here. I'm having quite a good time.'

'Yeah, it's all right,' Dave said, looking around smiling.

'I'm so glad we stopped. I feel a million times better now.'

Dave grunted a laugh, and put his cup of tea down.

'I keep on . . . having these phases where my mind just blanks out. Slipping in and out of consciousness.'

Jake looked at Dave's head. The smooth light brown oval was like a unique planet in the cafeteria, he thought.

The rows of grey plastic chairs and tables with bizarre pink and grey patterns on them, the people drinking their tea in front of the big windows, were like its solar system. Up there, no sleep for two days. Ideas and thoughts, revolving around him, hitting dark crud and stopping, aligning with our reality, then being off again. Sharing a different time span, a stretched, elongated conception of everything.

Jake watched in awe. Then his head fell down, suddenly faced with the smooth mottled grey surface of the plastic table. God, he couldn't handle it. He thought about how his bit of sleep had made him still connected to normality. He looked around. Like, what was going on here in this service station. He thought about how he never slept well. He wanted to be more in touch with the cycles of nature. I need to be, he thought.

'I'm so glad I got some sleep,' Jake said.

'Yes,' Dave answered, looking at him, and then his silver knife and fork chinked as he dropped them into the white porcelain plate, as again they both started laughing.

'So did nothing else happen?'

'No, not really . . . one of the cockneys had his stomach pumped.'

My God, thought Jake. Dave looked up, depressed.

'Yeah, I think Doudsy has got some answering to do.'

'Why?'

'Well, it was a pretty shit night,' Dave said, looking across the room with low eyes. 'Saying what a great party it was gonna be after that shit night.'

'I actually thought it was a good night. I mean, I know it wasn't a good night, the party wasn't very good, nor was Bristol. But,' he paused, 'I still had a good night. I mean it was funny. Well, it was this morning. You could write a story about this night,' Jake said, 'a short story.'

Dave shrugged and looked away, thinking Jake was joking.

'No, I'm serious, you could.'

Dave thought about it.

'I suppose you could, actually,' he said, and looked over his shoulder, shrugging, into his coat.

'Have you finished your coffee?'

Dave pointed to it, mouthing the word, 'Yeah.'

'Shall we go?'

Jake walked out of the toilet and looked down the glass hallway. The floor seemed to shimmer like a river. Dave was leaning against a phone booth. His hat over his eyes and his head hanging down, like a cowboy. As Jake walked past Dave his head swung around towards the door and they headed towards the exit.

harold wilson at
coombe lane

DOUGLAS GORDON

I LIKE THE SMELL OF TCP. Mum swabbed it on my knee. 'You're always in the wars,' she said.

It stung, but it was still good. She put on a plaster when she'd dried it.

'Going to show Dad,' I said. I ran down our hall, then remembered it was supposed to hurt so I limped the last bit.

He didn't look though. Mr Wattonstone was talking to him, frowning like it was something really important.

'Can you imagine it, Jack? Right here, in our own back yards.'

'What is?' I asked.

Mr Wattonstone looked. He said, 'Ever heard of the adage "children should be seen and not heard," young man?'

He's our Vicar. You never know when he's joking. He's got this really little nose, only his face is dead big and his forehead's really high.

I asked, 'What's in our back yard?'

'I doubt you'll be interested in the election,' the Vicar said.

It didn't make sense.

'The Labour Party,' Dad said, 'they're holding a meeting in Coombe Lane.'

I just looked.

Mt Wattonstone said, 'For grown-ups.'

– 'Why in the *school*, though?'

Coombe Lane's our old infants' school. It seemed stupid.

'Because they're publicly owned,' Dad said.

'Let this shower carry on and everything not nailed down will be publicly owned. Churches next, you mark my words, Jack. And that man's the *worst.*'

'*Who* is?' I asked.

'Harold Wilson,' Dad said.

I didn't get it. I frowned. I plumped down on our modern settee and picked at my plaster.

'When they've gone through the rest, they'll go for the churches,' the Vicar said.

I asked, 'You mean, Harold Wilson's coming to Coombe Lane?'

Then I felt stupid. I knew I'd sounded stupid. He's on the telly, in London.

Dad nodded. He was doing this little smile, I didn't know if it was cos of the Vicar or cos of me. 'Yes,' he said, 'right here.'

'Right in our own back yards.' Mr Wattonstone did a grin, too. 'Tell you one thing, Jack, I'll not have that lot parking on church grounds. They can stick their cars on the road, *I'm* locking the *gates.*'

'You know the Beatles come from Liverpool?'

Stephen Weatherup tutted. 'Everyone knows that.'

'I know,' I went, 'only I didn't know it was funny. That they come from Liverpool, and it's only in Lancashire.'

He blinked under his straggly fringe.

'So it's the same with Harold Wilson,' I said. 'Why's he coming *here?*'

He shrugged. 'Why shouldn't he?'

'Seems daft though. Coombe Lane.'

We'd walked along the stream across from the Vicarage. Some of the trees were coming in leaf, all bright and light, uncurling. We sat on the little grassy bandstand in the church field. The grass was wet on my bum. I lifted up my knees.

'Did you see on the news?' he asked.

I pulled back my plaster. You get white puffy skin like it's been in the bath too long. The scab looked soft. 'News is boring,' I said.

I watch 'Blue Peter' with John Noakes and Valerie Singleton and Peter Purvis. They've got a dog called Shep and another dog which I don't know what it's called. And 'Tomorrow's People', which is with children who've got a time machine, and it's like they're a secret special force. It's supposed to be dangerous, but you don't believe it because it's children and you know they can't do that. I like 'How!' with Fred Dineage, and on Fridays it's 'Crackerjack!' because they start with, 'If it's Friday, it must be *Crackerjack!*'

But when Dad watches news, I do something else.

'I know, but someone threw an *egg*,' Stephen said. 'Right at him. Right at Harold *Wilson*.'

We laughed loads.

I asked, 'Is *your* dad Conservative?'

'Everyone's is, aren't they?'

I picked at my scab. 'Did you know who was Prime Minister before Harold Wilson?'

'No. Did you know Garry Inch's dad's a councillor? At Parkridge.'

'Is he Con*serva*tive? So's mine! *Every*one's Conservative. Why does Harold Wilson think people want him *here?* *Nobody* wants him here!'

'I know,' he said.

I pushed at the pus so it splodged to the sides. You want to make it dry, then you can pick at it more, like all the little grazed bits round the edge.

I went, 'The Vicar doesn't. He can see right in the school, and that's where he's doing it.'

Stephen stuck his hands in his Parka pockets. 'D'you know what?' he said. 'We should get eggs.'

I looked at him, sucking my teeth cos I'd picked too much scab.

'Rotten eggs.' He grinned so his cheeks went puffy.

'To *throw* at him?'

'Yeah, then everyone'll know nobody likes him.'

We giggled again, but it was different.

'Stinkbombs, from that man's shop,' I snickered.

'No, eggs.' He twitched his fringe off his eyelash. 'So they splat.'

'Where'd we get *eggs*?'

He thought. 'Our mums' fridges?'

It didn't feel right. If I took eggs, it'd be stealing. I looked at him. He looked back, to see if we really meant it.

He asked, 'When's he coming?'

'Don't know.'

'You've got to find out.'

'Yeah,' I said. 'Or you can ask your dad.'

He shrugged. 'You can too. Are you going to look in your mum's fridge?'

'Don't know – yeah.' It wouldn't matter, it wasn't really real yet.

'You've got to,' he said.

'I know,' I went, 'so have you as well.'

I asked Mum, 'How d'you know if an egg's rotten?'

Then I felt guilty, cos I knew why I'd asked. My ears blushed.

'Is it for school?' she said.

'Um, just want to know. Are Uncle Tom's eggs ever rotten?' His chickens dig up Mum's flowerbeds, she's always shooing them off.

'Sometimes. Sometimes he leaves old eggs in the nest so they'll carry on laying.'

'He doesn't,' I went, 'he uses stone eggs.'

I knew cos I'd just looked.

She peered. 'Sometimes they've been there a lot longer than he thinks. Here. You can check 'em in a pan.'

She got this big saucepan and filled it with water.

'If they sink they're good, and if they float they're rotten. Or is it the other way? Fetch me an egg.'

I got two from these plastic holders in the fridge.

'Put 'em in, now. Gently.'

They settled. They went to the bottom, then stood up on their little ends.

I got excited. 'Are they rotten?'

'They're good,' she said.

I ran and got more. They next eggs did the same, then I went for another two. I tried them all, tutting, 'Mum, they're all *good.*'

She said, 'Sorry. I'll ask for spoiled ones next time, shall I?'

The doorbell rang. I dashed for it before Mum could get there. Stephen Weatherup was stood outside, with Garry Inch.

I just stared.

'Are you coming out then?' Stephen said.

I didn't know why Garry Inch was there. He'd never come to my house before. He stood back in the drive with his arms behind his back.

'Um, just be a minute.'

'Want to come in?' Mum asked. 'Is it not cold out?'

Stephen went, 'Think we'll wait outside, Mrs Burrage.'

I ran back again, pulling on a jumper, saying, 'Just going out, Mum!'

– 'Don't be back late,' she said.

Garry wouldn't turn round, he was backing up down the drive. Mum was still looking.

I whispered to Stephen, 'Why's he here?'

'Why shouldn't he be?'

'Thought it was just *us.*'

Stephen shrugged.

'Did you *tell* him?'

Mum shut the door.

'Where's yours?' Garry went, 'haven't you got any?' He swung his hands in front. He'd got these paper bags. He went, *'We've* got *loads.'*

My heart was thumping. 'Where did you get 'em?'

'Naylors,' Ste said, 'bought 'em coming back from school. Good, isn't it?'

It's where we get sweets. 'Didn't know they did eggs,' I said.

'Didn't you get any?'

My grin wouldn't come. 'Mum'd see them missing.'

Garry pulled a face. 'Have to give us money for some of these,' he said.

I whispered to Stephen, 'Thought it was just *us.'*

'Told Gaz at playtime,' he went. Loud, so Garry could hear. 'Want to look?'

We hid behind the garden wall. Garry put the bags on the frosty ground. He'd got a dozen eggs, fresh in two egg boxes. I had to give him pocket money. I felt scared, my hand shook fishing out this shilling and a thrupenny bit. I could see it in Stephen's face too, it was real now.

We ran over Fieldway and down along the stream. There were Vicarage lights on.

'Where can we chuck some then?' Garry asked. He darted his head all around, too excited.

'Should go up the Church Hall,' Ste said quietly. 'Hide 'em.'

We sneaked over the concrete footbridge, then up this path between the tennis courts and the Vicarage, running low so we wouldn't get seen.

The Church Hall was all dark. There's a path round its back side nobody goes on, leading up to Coombe Lane. There aren't any lights on it. There are brick steps going up, and black doors in the side of the hall.

'Makes you think of ghosts,' Ste said.

'You're *scared*,' Garry went.

'Go first then,' Ste told him.

Garry sniffed, 'I will.' Only he didn't.

It's dead narrow. There's the big hall on one side, and a tall wooden fence down the other with little scratchy bushes sticking out. We went up together. The iron railings were cold. The Church Hall seemed really big, it took a minute for your eyes to see it in the shadows. There's no windows this side, just bricks, and fat drainpipes, black and shiny.

Garry put the egg boxes down. 'Let's *chuck* one,' he said.

– 'It'll waste 'em.'

'Got *loads*.'

Ste went, 'Shouldn't we look, first? For if they're here yet?'

'Yeah,' I said, 'let's just go and look.'

We left the eggs in the dark by the railings.

There's holly bushes in front of this wall next to Coombe Lane. We sneaked up behind them. There are square brick shapes making holes in the wall, with stone roses, and gaps between the petals. I got down where I could see. A big street lamp opposite made everything orange. There were only a couple of men standing around outside the school.

'See, isn't *time* yet,' Garry said.

He was right. Not for ages. We went back to the eggs.

Garry got one out. He held it in his hand like a rock. 'Let's do 'em,' he said. He was standing like he was about to run or fight or something, a bit crouched, with his arm ready. He scowled when we didn't do it too. He acted like we had to, like it was a pact.

Ste leaned in and picked one out. I did as well, after. Then Garry chucked his egg. He really lobbed it! It splatted on the railings, there were runny bits left dripping, and bits of shell hanging off.

'*Go* on, do *yours*.'

I didn't want to though. I thought of Mr Wattonstone seeing the splats, looking really angry.

'Shouldn't waste 'em, Gaz,' Ste said.

'*Go* on, *chuck* it.'

Ste sighed. He turned and lobbed his at the wooden fence. You couldn't see it break in the shadows. The fence thrummed back.

'Now you,' Garry said.

'Who put you in charge?' I was really frowning. 'Anyway, shouldn't waste it.'

'Give it me then, *I'll* chuck it!'

He grabbed it out of my hand and lobbed it hard against the Church Hall wall.

It looked like vandalism, the way the egg splatted everywhere.

'Give us another.'

'*No*,' Ste said.

'You're both *use*less.'

'Just wasting 'em,' I went, 'you've broke mine already!'

He'd picked up another.

'Don't, Gaz, he's right,' Ste said. – 'Should save 'em for Harold Wilson.'

Garry was staring at me, still holding the egg.

Ste went, 'I'm right, aren't I?'

He still stared. Then his eyes flickered off. He sighed and said, 'S'pose so.' Then he threw it anyway, high on the wall where it cracked and ran like bird droppings. He laughed. 'How many's left now?'

– 'Eight,' Ste said.

'And *you've* chucked *three!*'

I'd shouted it. Ste's eyes darted towards the school.

'So somebody's only got two now.'

'Should have bought your own then,' Garry sneered.

I muttered, 'Paid for 'em, though.'

I could see Ste, frowning, blinking at Garry then blinking at me. 'We can take two each,' he said. 'Break the rest after.'

I'd looked off now, where I couldn't see Garry's face.

He muttered, 'Can't, can we? Not if we're legging it.'

– 'Tomorrow then,' Ste said. He picked up the second box and tucked it in his Parka. 'Might be nearly time, anyway.'

I stalked off in front with my back to them. My face felt really sour. I crunched right in front of the hall to the main gates, I didn't even bother hiding.

Then I just stood, looking. I'd forgot. I'd never seen them locked before. Mr Wattonstone had wound this chain round where the gates shut, and fixed it with this great big padlock.

Garry tutted behind, 'They're bl'ddy *locked*.'

We stared at them. I wasn't angry any more, I couldn't believe it.

'Could climb 'em,' I said. – 'S'pose.'

'Wall'd be better,' Ste said. 'Might be lower.'

We melted back from the light, sneaking into the hollies. We stood trying to think what to do, peering through the wall. Ste put his fingers in a gap in a rose.

'Will they fit?' he asked.

'What, the eggs? Might.'

Garry went, 'Give them us then.'

Stephen got one from inside his Parka. He tried it, you could make it fit. He said, 'Two of us should go over and one'll have to pass 'em through.'

I thought about it. 'Yeah, behind our backs.'

'Me then,' Garry said, 'I'll stay back so you lot don't break 'em.'

We stood there. Nobody climbed. Ste handed Garry the eggs. Then I just started, and Ste climbed up as well. I thought the men would look when my head went over the top. I thought they might shout cos of trespassing, but they were all just waiting for Harold Wilson. I didn't even have to jump, I could climb down.

I'd never seen these men before. Not any of them.

'Do you know anyone?' I asked Ste.

'Um – might not come from Seddonfield,' he said. 'Cos of all our dads vote Conservative.'

Garry hissed behind, 'Stick your hands back. Which one's who?'

I wiggled my fingers through a gap in a rose.

'Here, Gaz,' Ste said next to me.

I stared at the men. I felt an egg in my fingers. My heart was really thumping.

'Who've I give it to? Have you got it?'

I lowered my hand to the front. Nobody at the school seemed to notice. The men looked grainy in the orange light, peering up the road or pacing with their coats pulled tight, smoking cigarettes. They didn't care, we were only kids. I put the egg in my pants pocket. They'd parked their cars on the pavements, all up and down, like Mr Watton-stone said they'd have to. Only not by the school gates, so Harold Wilson could still stop. I palmed my second egg in my other pocket.

'Take mine too,' Garry hissed, 'and don't break 'em!'

We heard him scramble. His egg was cold in my hand. Then he thumped off the end of the wall and sauntered up to Ste. This man in a long coat peered at us a bit too long. Then he just looked off again.

'Hand us me eggs then.'

My tummy felt tight, like I wanted to run away. I didn't really want Garry holding eggs. I'd have to give him them though. *'Here.'* I nudged Ste's hand with mine. 'Pass 'em on.'

The men looked grey and fuzzy. More kept coming up, milling around. There was just us on our side. I kept my hands in the tops of my pockets, pushing them open so my eggs wouldn't squash. The eggs got warm and my palms started sweating.

'Could hide under the concrete bridge,' I said. My voice sounded little and thin. 'After.'

'How'd we *get* there, stupid? Gate's *locked*.'

'Um – Vicar's front gate's never locked.'

I go through it sometimes coming home from school. They don't mind. If Sara Wattonstone's outside, I talk to her, so it's nice.

Ste went, 'Through the *Vica*rage?' He shook his head. '*Can't*.'

'Why?'

'Cos of the *Vicar*.'

I stared at him. I hadn't thought. Everyone's scared of the Vicar. It's cos he booms when he talks, and he's really big. Only I never think of it, cos I go in their drive all the time. When the Vicar makes his jokes, Sara Wattonstone just tuts and ignores him.

'He'll *see* us,' Ste said.

'You're just *stu*pid,' Garry went.

I huffed, 'Well you shouldn't go smashing eggs against the Church Hall, should you?'

Nobody said anything.

'So what d'you want to do?'

– 'Have to climb back,' Ste said.

'They'll *catch* us.'

Garry went, 'Won't if we're faster.'

I glanced at Ste. He shrugged. 'Dunno,' he mumbled.

Over the road, the men were craning their necks.

I moaned, 'Should go through the Vicar's *gate*.'

My breath puffed out in a cloud. I watched it. I shivered. It was going to happen soon.

Ste asked, really quiet, 'Do you still both want to do it then?'

You could hear us all breathing.

– 'Don't know,' I said.

You can't be first to back out, or then they can blame you for it.

'Gaz?' Ste asked.

He didn't say anything. My eggs felt hot and slippy in my palms.

Then Harold Wilson's big black car was coming. You knew it was his, it had to be, it looked really important cos he's Prime Minister. It slowed down right by the school. My hand was shaking. I had the egg in it, I'd pulled it out of my pocket. I didn't know what I was going to do. I thought it might crack. The car was just there, and everyone shuffling and moving about. A man got out, then another, and it was Harold Wilson! You knew, cos of his raincoat, only he didn't have his pipe in his hand like on the telly. He sort of hunched and turned his back in the crowd. He was gone through the middle and they all just shuffled in round him. It was really quick!

Garry was craning his neck. 'Did you see him? Was it *him*?'

Ste said, '*Yeah* – um – dunno.'

'*Must* have been,' I said, 'he had on his raincoat.'

'Could you have got a shot off?' Garry was jumping, trying to see over the men. 'I didn't know it was *him*. Could you *see* him?'

'Dunno. He was just gone – '

We started going, '*Kuh – tuh*,' acting like we were really disappointed. Only I'd known, just when he came, that our dads wouldn't really want us throwing eggs at Harold Wilson. And I knew I wouldn't have really done it. We were just acting disappointed so we could still pretend.

Ste said, 'He'll be inside for *hours*, Gaz.'

'Can still wait.'

Ste sighed. 'I want to go *home*.'

I handed Garry my eggs. We didn't have to hide them, there wasn't anyone left to see. When I'd climbed over the wall, he rolled them through the gaps. I couldn't find the egg box.

We kicked at the stiff holly leaves, pretend-disappointed.

Ste said, 'We should throw 'em anyway. Shouldn't we? See what it might have been like.'

We traipsed back down the path. Garry started aiming at the wall, only Ste went, 'Don't chuck it at the hall, Gaz, me dad does Boy's Brigade! Might be him has to clean it *up*.'

'Bloody useless,' Garry Inch went. He flung his egg on the ground right in front of him. It splatted back on his shoes. We didn't laugh.

'Take this, Harold Wilson,' Ste said. But quiet. He threw his eggs at the ground, where birds might get them in the morning, or a hedgehog, or it might rain and wash them away.

I could feel my arm do a pathetic throw. My egg just cracked and dribbled its stuff on the steps. My second didn't break at all. I had to go and get it and throw it again.

We looked where we'd done it, next night, just me and Ste. It was dark. We couldn't really see anything. We only looked over the steps for a second.

'Don't think there's anything there now,' he said, and we turned and ran away again.

an uncut diamond

DONNA GRAY

FROM THE OUTSIDE Carolyn looked disgusting. Not someone you'd want to say hello to in a million years. She
walked around untidy and in a daze all the time. Describing
Carolyn as a drenched mouse or a sensa fowl that's been hit
with a wet towel seems cruel for anyone, but the truth isn't
pretty.

Outside appearances lead people astray and that's
exactly what happened in Carolyn's case. As the days
turned into weeks and weeks into months, Carolyn started
to fit in with the prison regime, but not with any grace or
airs. But she was fitting in none the less.

Elder couldn't remember when she started noticing
Carolyn, but she did, and Carolyn began to grow on her.
Carolyn's first positive step came when she got the job in
the garden in October of last year. She took a back seat at
work and did whatever was asked of her. Her low self-
esteem led her to accept anything that was said and done to
her, good, bad or nasty. And in her environment nastiness
was oozing. But she took it one day at a time; she wasn't in
any rush. Carolyn held her head down and did her bit as
best as she could.

The garden party where Carolyn worked was like a
haven. Even though the girls did the most dirty work, they

never seemed to get fed up. The leftover food got thrown out of the windows with the jam-rags – you name it, it all went out of the windows, and had to be cleaned up. But there was a good side as well. Carolyn and the rest of the girls were responsible for the upkeep of the trees and flowers on the ground. The flowers beautified the yard from all angles.

The garden party managers were Miss Stewart and Mr Mac. Miss Stewart rolled around the grounds making sure everything was ship-shape, and Mr Mac rocked around the yard. He didn't smile often but when he did you'd done well. Neither manager went by outside appearances; even if you were old and machetted, they'd accept you. As the prison population turned over, so people came and went. The more senior Red Bands all went to other places. Soon Carolyn's opportunity came to get her Red Band.

Elder turned up on Thursday afternoon a week before Christmas and her eyes caught the Red Band hanging round Carolyn's neck. The Red Band meant Carolyn could move around to and from work without being escorted.

'Oh, Carolyn, you've got your licence for the crew,' said Elder. Carolyn laughed.

'I'll be running with the big girls now,' said Carolyn.

'About time,' said Slosh, the most senior Red Band in the garden.

Slosh took Carolyn under her wing and the two became great friends. When Elder was there part-time the three were inseparable, but they got their work done. As the three months whizzed by Carolyn became more confident and settled in even better. Carolyn excelled at whatever she did, mowing the yard, cutting edges and planting. She wanted things to change when she got out, and she made every effort.

And she got a bigger push in that direction. Miss Stewart and Security gave Carolyn the job outside the prison gate, cleaning, planting and cutting the edges on the drive approaching the prison entrance. That was a big step, as it was only the most trusted that got that job.

One afternoon when Carolyn wasn't working outside, Elder went to work. Carolyn saw Elder coming. 'Are you with us this afternoon?' she asked.

'Yes,' said Elder.

'Superwoman is here,' Carolyn shouted to the rest of the girls, and they all laughed.

'And she loads the skip if she's plugged in, stay clear of her,' Carolyn said. And the girls laughed again.

The fun in the shed was non-stop. The shed was the nerve-centre of the garden. Tools, clothes and all the bits and bobs went down in the shed. It was furnished to depict its surrounding flowers in each corner. Each girl had a chair and cupboard space for her boots and gloves. And there was a hi-fi on the table next to Carolyn's chair. You had to work hard in the garden, but whatever you did was appreciated.

Carolyn kept coming out of her shell and sometimes Elder didn't even recognise her. At times Carolyn still looked scruffy, her clothes still hanging badly. But Slosh kept getting her back in contention. Apart from Carolyn getting annoyed when people digged her about how much baccy she put in her Rizla for making a roll-up, nothing got on Carolyn's nerves; she was laid back.

Carolyn's children came to visit from time to time. Her mothering skills, though, left a lot to be desired. But like all mothers in prison, she always believed she was no good. Generally mothers were hard on themselves for leaving their kids to fend for themselves. Carolyn was no different. Three out of her six children were on her pin-board. Beautiful children they were. Carolyn always had a smile when she spoke about her kids.

Carolyn's work got better and better, and she thought her time got easier. Everything was falling into place. In May, Carolyn sat the board for home leave. No problems. Everyone celebrated with her when she was told she had four days out. Carolyn, Slosh and two other girls shared the same dorm. Whenever Elder passed, she had to stop and say hello to the garden party and gave Slosh and Carolyn their kiss. Elder thought Carolyn had really grown on her. Their dorm was the business! They had music, games and overall respect for each other. Everyone wanted to be in Carolyn and Slosh's dorm.

A few days went by and Elder hadn't gone by the girls' wing. On day four, Elder stopped by the food hatch in the cell door to peer through, and Carolyn's bed was empty.

'Elder!' said Slosh with a welcoming screech. She came over and got her kiss.

'Where is Carolyn?' asked Elder.

'She's gone on her home leave,' said Slosh with a big grin. 'And you know what she's getting up to.'

'Nuff sex,' said Elder. And everyone's eyes said it all. They wished they were anywhere but here in prison.

Carolyn came back buzzing. She had it all sorted. She was oozing with self-esteem. Now nothing would be able to touch Carolyn. But even with the best intentions, you can find yourself in ruts. Carolyn found this out in a bad way and it knocked the wind out of her sails.

Carolyn got mandatory drugs tested. And the news wasn't good when the test came back. Carolyn got a positive for a substance not even she could pronounce the name of. All that Carolyn had worked so hard for came tumbling down like a deck of cards. Carolyn was to have gone home in three weeks with all her achievements intact, but she had lost everything. Her Red Band job and all trust for working outside the gate had disappeared. Carolyn went down the block as a punishment, and got seven days added to her sentence. The garden girls weren't best pleased. They cried and wanted to go on strike for Carolyn.

'How can that be?' they kept asking.

They couldn't believe she could have been that stupid. They all talked about not doing anything when they got home leave. It did seem that Carolyn was not strong enough.

Elder heard what had happened and went to see what was going on. Carolyn was upset, but not as upset as the garden girls, which seemed odd to Elder.

'What happened?' asked Elder.

Carolyn explained, but not with a lot of conviction. Elder smelled a rat, but prisoners have to stick together. And Elder couldn't help having a nagging thought that Carolyn knew more than she was letting on. But Elder wasn't going to judge her.

Everyone felt it when Carolyn was put on all sanctions and got taken off the wing with television and her best mates. But all sanctions meant back to basic, and that's where Carolyn was at, back to Square One. Miss Stewart, she fought each and every case when things like this happened. But there was nothing she could have done. She had to take all she had given Carolyn away from her. It can't have been easy.

Slosh was Carolyn's oldest friend. She thought that Carolyn had been set up. Things were happening too quickly. And it didn't seem as if Carolyn was getting the benefit of the doubt. But in life sometimes you only get one chance, and it seemed that Carolyn had blown hers.

It seemed that Carolyn's home leave had caused her to lose everything.

Elder saw Carolyn a few days after she had been taken off the posh wing. She was in Education. A smile that didn't reach her eyes, her shoulders stooped, everything about her negative. And Elder wanted to cry. Carolyn put on a brave face. But sadness had taken its residence and the rent was all paid up.

Even though Carolyn had been dealt these terrible blows she wasn't hiding away. She deserved full marks for that. For the next few weeks whenever Elder saw Carolyn it was on exercise or in Education. Carolyn put a front on, but her smiles never quite reached her eyes.

Elder met Carolyn on the Sunday of the week she was due to be released.

'It is soon, now, Carolyn,' said Elder.

'Friday,' said Carolyn.

'I bet you're happy to go home,' said Elder.

'I can't wait,' said Carolyn.

Elder saw Carolyn in passing for the remainder of the week. Thursday night before Carolyn went on Friday, Elder went by Slosh's dorm and asked for her.

'She's gone to see Carolyn before she goes tomorrow,' said Buncie.

'Oh sugar!' said Elder.

She meant to see Carolyn that evening as well, but it slipped her mind and she couldn't turn back because it wouldn't go down well with the staff. However well you got on with the staff you couldn't take it for granted you wouldn't get into trouble, so Elder had to go to her wing. Come tomorrow, Carolyn would be home with her family. Good on her!

Everything went on as usual inside the fifty-foot red brick walls. Elder went on her part-time job in the garden on Saturday, the day after Carolyn had gone. Elder and Slosh were pruning the roses.

'Have you heard anything from Carolyn?' Elder asked Slosh.

'No,' said Slosh.

'Haven't you phoned her yet?' asked Elder.

'Carolyn lives on the street,' said Slosh. 'Cardboard City Street!'

It took a while to sink in for Elder. She looked at Slosh, dumbfounded and in disbelief.

'So how did she get released? Didn't she need a home address before the prison would release her?' Elder didn't understand and she left it at that. It didn't seem that Slosh wanted to speak about it.

Elder was at work, that was her full-time work in the staff shop. She had a visit from an officer, Honey, and that was when she heard the sad news.

'Carolyn OD'd,' Honey said.

'*Caka fart mirast cloth*!' Elder shouted. 'Wah yu sa?'

Honey started again. 'Carolyn – '

'Do you mean Carolyn Kennedy who went home last Friday?'

'Was it Friday she went home? I don't know. She used to work outside the gates,' Honey said.

'That's Carolyn,' Elder said.

'What does that mean? Is she in hospital?' asked Elder.

'No,' said Honey. 'When you overdose you're dead.'

Elder's eyes welled up with tears.

'How long had she been out?' asked Honey.

'Seven days,' said Elder. She was racking her brain to remember how may Fridays ago it was. It all seemed too soon. The sad truth was that Carolyn died only a week and a day ago.

Honey was a bit cocky, as if yet again the officers had been proved right. When everything was taken off Carolyn they knew time would tell and Elder wanted to scream, but it wouldn't have helped.

Elder went to look for the girls in the shed but it was empty. The grounds were deserted apart from a few girls doing exercise. Elder was in shock for the rest of the day as the whole prison was buzzing with the news. The people who knew Carolyn best for the two years she'd been inside grieved.

'Come unto me, my children, and I will give you rest.' It was Sunday and Elder went to church with Carolyn on her mind. Elder dreaded to think how Miss Stewart was going to take it when she came off her long weekend. Through the grapevine she had heard Mr Mac and the girls had prayed yesterday. Mr Mac was beside himself with grief. This time, Elder was thinking, she could empathise with an officer.

Before the service got to the main sermon, Rosie, the chaplain, spoke about Carolyn's death. 'I don't know how many of you remember Carolyn Kennedy, who worked in the garden, but the prison was contacted with news of her death. She died the same afternoon of her release. Her sister wants me to say thanks for all the support Carolyn received while inside the prison. She is at peace now. Her sister also wanted to say her sister had the happiest times here in prison.'

Heckles, sighs and grunts filled the church. What must be going through people's minds – Carolyn died the same day she was released.

The service went on for the next hour. Elder couldn't wait for it to be over and two o'clock to come. Elder needed to see Slosh. Carolyn died the same day she went out – it couldn't be.

She went to find Slosh.

'Slosh, did you know Carolyn died the same day she went out?' Elder asked.

'Yes,' she answered.

Some days later, Slosh gave Elder some more insight into Carolyn's last days before she went home. Carolyn didn't think she'd cope outside the prison walls. But how could that be, thought Elder. People should be jumping through hoops gagging to get home.

Elder's wig curled when she heard how Carolyn cried because she didn't want to leave the prison. It saddened Elder to hear that Carolyn's life was that bad outside. Elder learned that Carolyn intended to finish with her boyfriend, even though that didn't go in Carolyn's favour. If the newspaper was to be believed, he was responsible for her death.

The headline in the paper read: 'Boyfriend Arrested: Woman Found Dead'. And a paragraph from the newspaper in Peterborough, Cambridge:

'A woman's body was found lying beneath the bridge. Hundreds of people went about their weekly shop at the riverside Asda supermarket as the drama unfolded, unaware that nearby, across the river, police were cordoning off the tragic scene.'

Elder read the clipping over and over. She went over what Slosh had told her of Carolyn's overall situation. All

Elder had seen and heard of Carolyn she put to the back of her mind in the weeks after her death. Elder wanted to remember Carolyn as the smiling bubbly person she was within these fifty-foot walls. The Carolyn that made you laugh with her silly antics.

Not all of us who go through a difficult time can keep on fighting. Not many will understand what Carolyn had to cope with in that one day. Maybe Carolyn didn't want drugs in her life any more. Maybe she couldn't face the pressures that life has to offer any more. Carolyn had seen life without drugs, without physical and emotional abuse, and she wanted it, but maybe she didn't think she was strong enough to get it on her own . . . Maybe, in what should be the godforsaken hole of prison, Carolyn found love; people who care; people who understand. Maybe Carolyn wanted to break the cycle. And she did it the only way she knew how. She didn't want to be a junkie any more.

Hundreds of people inside and out can empathise. Let's not forget Carolyn's children. They might not understand now what happened to their mum. But when they do, they should take comfort from this short look at her.

She was an uncut diamond.

the mating game

FATIMA KASSAM

'IN THE LONG-TERM

'*Happy, solvent, homely, caring, well-educated Hindu businessmen who enjoys travel, cinema, countryside seeks similar female for friendship, relationship and maybe more in the long-term in Central London area.*'

Farah picks up the phone and dials, her voice full of excitement and anticipation.

'Hi. I'm Farah. A British Asian woman copy-writer living in London. I'm Muslim, not Hindu. I love movies, swimming, and as I'm a bit plump I go to the gym. If you like the sound of me get in touch. My phone number is 0207 937 9596 and I too live in central London.'

Farah tosses and turns, dreaming of her prince-to-be. She gets up lazily and makes her dose of café noir, goes back to the real world of copy-writing. Thank God she is self-employed. No Circle Line due to fire fighters' strike – London Underground did not want to put the public's life in jeopardy, as if it already wasn't.

At midday, as Farah bemoans the trials and tribulations of the Circle Line to herself, the phone rings. Farah picks it up in a state of nonchalance.

'Hi, I'm Dilip from "Meet your Mate". I'm Hindu, born and brought up in India. I went to St Vincent's Roman Catholic School. What about you?'

'I'm a true Brit, Londoner through and through,' Farah replies, trying to put on the North London accent her role models like Meera Syal had.

Dilip continues in the same self-obsessed way. 'I'm now established here. You sound like a modern but traditional girl. Would you like to meet?'

Farah's head is confused by the contradiction in terms, but musters up: 'Well, if we meet it has to be somewhere in public.'

Dilip tries to be sophisticated but is marred by the fact that he is 37 going on 137. 'What about the sushi bar in Selfridge's? How about tomorrow?' Farah comes in with 'No, Thursday at 4 p.m.,' trying to throw him off guard, ensuring her safety with the pre-Christmas shoppers. 'OK, ciao,' he replies before she can say 'Bye.'

Farah worries about whether she is doing the right thing, answering an advert. Yet she feels age, time and life in general are passing her by. She needs to take a risk. He could be genuine. He is educated, knows about business and the real world. On the other hand he could be out for 'kicks' or extra-marital sex. Just wanting to experience sex with a different woman, like a hobby.

Two days seem like a hellish eternity engulfed with loneliness to Farah as she muses on her prince. Finally, Thursday arrives and she's in Selfridge's an hour early with rape alarm well-positioned in a purple handbag.

As she looks at all the different coffees near the sushi bar a short, well-endowed man with thick hair and a matching moustache arrives. 'Farah,' says this sweaty blazer-and-grey-trousers type. Her heart sinks. In the flesh Dilip is over-weight, short and ugly. She is reminded of Dan Jeremy, the porno star.

'Oh, Dilip,' she says trying to be civil.

'Welcome to my corner shop,' he retorts, sensing her unease.

As they chat over coffee, Farah asks, 'Tell me about your-self and your family.'

He replies with a smile, 'I've got one sister younger than me. I'm 37 and she's 31. Our parents had us late after ten years of marriage.'

Farah laughs, 'I'm four years older than you. I'm 41 and do not want children.'

He moves his fingers to his lips and exclaims: ' I don't want to know anything more about you until you *vow* to see me again.' Farah suddenly turns from humble Asian woman to assertive in-your-face. 'I'm English – don't mess with me!' she commands.

The ride home from Selfridge's to Kensington seems very lonely to a woman who, while part of the thriving, accessible city, always feels apart. She decides to call Dilip to thank him. A second meeting is proving very difficult to set up due to her apprehension of Dilip. The porno star is in her mind but need for love gets the better of her as she fan-tasises about having a man in her life, and the crushing lonely feeling swells in her heart.

On Sunday Dilip rings Farah and says he wants to see her. Farah tries putting him off, but finally gives in as Dilip gives her an ultimatum and she needs to see if this will work. He tells her, 'This is the trouble with you, every time I try to get close to you, you retreat. This is the last time I'm letting you be my tortoise.' Sensing he is about to put the phone down, Farah interjects: 'You're vegetarian. I thought that they were patient and slow to act.'

Dilip laughs, 'Can I come now?'

Farah hesitates but gives in with an 'OK then!'

Half an hour later he is in her flat. There is an awkward silence. It feels like he is coming to visit his mistress. She offers him a drink, spilling it all over herself. 'What's in there?' he asks and takes her by the hand into the bedroom. He undresses her and pulls her towards him. He sits on the bed as she says, 'I think this is going too fast for me. Dilip, no, no, don't,' she screams as she begins to freeze up.

'No, what, don't hurt me, Farah.'

Farah is frozen as Dilip lies on the bed, holds her firmly down with both hands pressing on her breasts. She screams, 'Don't hurt me.' He pulls his hands away, lightly presses his right hand over her mouth, parts her legs on his shoulders and penetrates her hard and rough, again, again and again. Dilip then proceeds to get dressed, as Farah puts on a dressing gown in a state of numbness. He dances around the room with her, holds her hand before departing to meet a friend.

Farah, in total shock, stares at the TV screen which is displaying a nature programme, 'The Mating Game'. It shows two turtles mating in the animal kingdom and then returning to their separate, solitary lives. She feels completely violated and humiliated with rape, throws the remote so hard at the TV screen that it shatters the glass to bits, and stares at the pieces on the floor, cutting into the carpet – messy, bloody, alone, like her.

lost in one's thoughts

DENESE KEANE

SARAH, THIS GIRL, she needed some excitement in her life. She wanted much more than life could give her. Down by the beach one hot and windy summer day Charlie lay there expecting something good to happen to him. He was just laying there sipping his juice and smoking his tobacco. This man was a famous and glamorous person so he was looking for a lot of enjoyment to go with. Life is precious and good, so he had to make the most of it. This girl was a fool to life, happiness she need, some one to bring her out of her shell and let her see the world from a different angle.

So nice and shy, she strolls along on the beach but there and then her stroll carried her through the wind. The splendid moves of her body made him want her more, but all her attention was where the music was coming from, it made her smile with radiant light. She stop for a while as he look at her. His heart gave a sudden beat and he wonder to himself if he could dare. Dare to love, dare to keep her only for his self, but the sound of the music mix with wind carried his thoughts afar off. Carried away with his thoughts he stare at mountains from where he was thinking what it would be like having her.

He thought dinner under candlelight, flowers in her vase, champagne with bubbles to burst and laughter to cheer. Oh what a wonder life it would be and his thoughts went on and on, but the heavy drops of rain took him back to earth where he had to hurry and pack his stuff. He began to run but stop for a while and saw her standing from the balcony. She watched the lightning dancing to the bass rumble of thunder. She suddenly realise she was being watch by a passing stranger, out of nowhere. Shy and young at heart, she ran indoor, to look out through a window in a distance on her unknown admirer.

He smile with such joy at how she ran as a child at play. But he then carried on, while the rain soak his pack he had with him. Reaching his summer home, he stumble across a pair of slippers, with a handful of sea shell along it too. The first thing came across his mind, someone was playing on his verandah, and in the sudden downpour of the rain they must have run off. Without giving it much thought, he went indoor to get his soak wet clothes off, to new fresh clothes. The evening went off really quickly and so the night falls, the skies went real clear and pretty.

With his neighbours nearby with fireworks and dancers, everyone from near came out to gather around, to warm up to the lovely night atmosphere and the night enjoyment which is in high spirit until late midnight. Everyone mixing with the smooth atmosphere and drinking their drinks of their likeness. The dancers entertaining them, it's a lovely summer night under the moon and starlight from above. But he wander off in his own company, down the sea shore in search of a moment to be alone, to ease his mind a bit, from all the world's hassle and worries.

He reach to a distance, where is only him alone in sight, he then sit on a tree's trunk, and sip his drink with pleasure. To the sound of the sea thrash against the shore and the music from a distance of the night's outdoor entertainment. He found a piece of stick and began to mark in the wet sea sand, under his foot. Bore stiff of just sitting alone he began his way back, taking him nearer to the night event, but he went off to his home, so he took off his shoes and walk barefoot back up his path. He saw a shadow movement in a flash to the side of the house. He follow on, only to see the shy and playful at heart girl, holding the slippers in her hands.

He ask, 'What's you doing here, away from the rest?' but she hang her head in silence with no word to answer. So he ask her to come back, to the front of the house, she reluctantly walk towards him, but reaching near she attempt to run, but he reach out for her. She gave out a large scream, but with all the music, no one heard her cry. He explain he would not hurt her, but she twist and fight, as a wild animal in fear of its life. But she soon realise her fight and twist was in vain, so she finally gave up. Then he slowly release her from his strong embrace, but not fully, he still hold her hands, she would not look her stranger kidnapper in the face. So he slowly raise her cheek to see her face. Her eyes shine in the moonlight, but she was still far too shy to keep a straight face for long. She beg him to release her arm but he would not, he demand she explain what she was doing around his home at this time of the night.

But she was lost for words, so he ask, 'So these slippers are yours.' She shook her head. He said, 'Okay, fine, how comes they are here in the first place?' Still no answer. He then said, 'They were there when I came in earlier in the evening, were you there earlier on?' She shook her head in reply. He then remind her he won't hurt her one way or the other. But she was still shaking with fear. He ask her if she would like to sit down for a while. But in Sarah's mind she just want to be free. She seems willing, so Charlie and Sarah sat on the steps, when out came a cat, rubbing on Sarah's sides. He said, 'Oh! Is this your cat?' He smile and took the cat up in his arms.

He said, 'Do you come around here much?' She still insist on not saying a word, still stroking the cat with lovely strokes. He ask, 'Would you come in for a drink? And the cat seems hungry.' She raise to her feet and he did too, he lead the way in and she follow with the cat running in between. He went to the kitchen and took out cat food in a tin, open it and feed the cat. And ask her what she would love to drink, she smile and said, 'Nothing thanks, please.' He fix himself a drink and soon sit himself down at the table in the kitchen. But she watch the cat as he ate his meal.

Then she sudden come out, 'I have to go now.' He said, 'Will I see you again?' But she stick to her shy and innocent smiles. He watch her, she leave and disappear into the night. But again she ran off, leaving her slippers this time inside, so Charlie knew she would be back for sure. Soon it was dawn, he goes running on the shore, early in the morning. He run past her home, where he saw her, but no one to see in sight. He took a swim after his morning runs, he walk slowly up to his home, she was there waiting to see him. But why so early in the morn?

He came up, sat beside her, but she move a bit to the side of the step where she sat. He gave a loud laugh and ran his hand through his hair, in the way how she has been acting. But he then stood and went indoor, she follow him. She could not go in this morn, he had realise when he was not around she would invite herself in, so he close the door with his keys this time around. He offer her breakfast which she gladly accept but still, being shy and all, he fetch the cat some meal too, and he sat having his coffee too. He try to make conversation, but she was more interested in getting her slippers. But he had already remove them to a more secret place where he thought she will not look. But he would not say anything as he watch her look and search in vain. After a while, making her start to wonder, he said, 'Have you drop something, my dear? But what's your name?' She said 'Oh! It is just Sarah,' as if she did not care what it was, as if it meant nothing to her.

'Oh! Sarah dear, what's it you search for?' She said, 'I swear I left it.' Hearing this he said, 'Swear what?' She said, 'I swear I left my slippers here, yesterday.' He said, 'You are sure?' She seems a bit worried now, he could see it in her eyes. He said, 'It is only slippers,' She snap, 'Yes! It is my only slipper. Please let me have it.' He said, 'If only you would spend the day in my company.' She said she had to go by eight o'clock to be on her way. He said, 'To where?' She said, 'To my work.' He said, 'What kind of work?' She said, 'I clean a bar in town and I have to walk to get there.' He laugh, but Sarah did not find it funny. It was her only way of living.

He said, 'Where in town do you work?' She explain, but he carry on, 'I never see you there before.' But she answer very angrily, 'I am just a cleaner.' He then saw it was not a very pleasant experience for her doing cleaning. So he told her to forget the job for a while, but she said, 'How could I? I need to work to survive, don't you think anyone need to do just that?' 'Just forget about the stupid job, Sarah, for a while.' '*Yes*! If I do how would I survive then?' He ask, 'Would you trust me, if I say I would take care of you?'

Sarah laugh and say, 'But why? You don't even know me, and what's your name by the way?' 'Well, friends call me Charlie,' but before he could finish she said, 'Charlie!' in surprise, 'That's the name of the bar I clean up in town. Don't tell me . . .' and he laugh and say, 'Yes I am.'

'But I never met you before.' 'No you won't, my brother runs my business. But I am the man behind the business. OK, Sarah. So stop worrying about the stupid job now for a while, will you?' 'Yes, but today is my wage day, anyway.' But he continue, 'For the last time, Sarah, let go your hair and sit back for a while, will you, and let me take care of you for a while, OK?' She gave a loud sigh in sign of relief and agree after all and say, 'OK, boss.' He said in a very sharp tone, 'Never ever call me boss ever again. My name is Charlie, OK, Sarah?' She said, 'OK, sorry, Charlie.' He said, 'No need to be sorry, just call me Charlie.'

So he took up his mobile and rang someone, had a brief conversation and short. Then he ask her what size she wore, she said seven, he said, 'Follow me.' He took her down a hallway, through a door which lead on to another room, stock with women clothing of all sort. She said, 'What you got here, a clothes department or what?' He said, 'I run more than one kind of business, OK my love?' She said, 'No one has ever called me my love before. Why,' she said, 'you call me that?' He said, 'In time you will know.' He said, 'Help yourself to anything your heart desire, my love.' She smiles in wild surprise, not ever seen anything like this before. She did not waste time, she pick one set, he said, 'That's all, pick some more while you are at it, my dear.' So she did as Charlie has instruct her to do.

He directs her to a well design bathroom with everything a woman could ever need for one's comfort. He told her,

'When you are finish and dress, you know where to find me, OK my love, Sarah.' He then went off to another room up the hallway, and came out and slip a brown envelope under the bathroom door. In no time she was out and he follow behind to get himself ready also. They left together in his car, to go into town, he took her to change her cheque. She was very much please with the figures on the cheque. He took her to the beauty salon, and for lunch in this expensive restaurant, he went to get a steam bath and carried her along with him, then a massage after. It was a day well spent with not a penny of hers spent. On reaching back he ask her, 'How do you feel after all of this?' She was lost for words completely.

They went in. She hurry to find her cat. She feed the cat, and rest in the suite in the living room, a bit tired, she start to doze off. When Charlie invite her upstairs, he ask her to go rest comfortable in one of the guest room. With home a distance off, she was not up for the journey. She's out in no time, he settle down beside her, she round and throw her arm around him, whatever she was now dreaming she was in quite a bit of content at heart. She was woken later on in the night by the patter of raindrops on the roof and the sudden cold breeze blowing through the open window with small raindrops coming in. She jump in such fright and Charlie only turn, she came back to bed and went under the cover, she drew near to Charlie's side, he turn back around to her, he kiss her on the forehead, and hug her in his big strong arms.

It was five o'clock in the morning now, and woken by the clock ding-donging, he woke, so did she, but he try to leave out of his close embrace with her, but she held on tight to him instead. It was his time of morning to go jogging, but he was capture by Sarah's warmness of longing to be loved. How could he resist her, after calling her my love and my dear, so he forgot about his jogging, he had no way of getting away. He try to explain what he does in the morn, but she would not let go of him one way or another. He had capture her first in his arms one night, not long ago, told her to forget her stupid job, now it is time to capture him in his own space, let him know he must forget his jogging for the morning and just focus on her, as he said she should let him take care of her. And so the amazing thrill of two people from two different walks of life is now trap in each other's world. Will it go on, will it end? The truth is yet untold of these two different amazing new lives which has just begun, in an unremarkable way. Seems like destiny has kiss them both with the undeniable faith of love.

emine's fight

AYDIN MEHMET ALI

'LOOK AT EMINE . . . she doesn't have a worry in the world!'

Emine has let herself go to the rhythm of the music. A high-pitched female's voice lamenting the loss of her love, cursing her luck, while the instruments are moving into a frenzy of movement inviting the hips to gyrate, the breasts to shake, the arms to stretch forward, the head slightly tilted back moving in sync with the body. But the hips are out of control. They are rolling and shaking as though they have a life of their own, as though they are not attached to a body.

Emine has tied a bright red embroidered *yemeni* around her hips, extenuating the belly-dance movements. She is happy. Her eyes are shining, her mouth in perpetual laughter. Every now and again the eyebrows become knitted, the look intense, the lips pursed. Emine is concentrating on the movement of the body in tune with the music. She stops on the same spot, one foot on tiptoe, her hips making huge, provocative, sensuous swings, sharp swings and back again towards that direction. Another woman comes up to her and reciprocates the movement. She swings her hip and brushes against Emine's hip. Emine laughs, laughs to her heart's content and moves off.

She feels eighteen or is it sixteen? Light-headed. Light-bodied. Not a care in the world . . . Emine dreams of being young, of being loved, of being the shining moon . . . no one can touch her. She is the most beautiful in the village. The most desired. The subject of sweet dreams, painful dreams, wet dreams, nightmares! Emine . . . who doesn't give them the time of day. Emine the wild fawn. Emine the untouchable! The wild one. With beautiful eyes. And a heart-shattering heart. Who will she marry? Who will she choose? Oh! Emine, oh! My wild Emine! My beauty! My dove!

Emine dances at her sister's wedding. The whole village is at the wedding. Young men watch. Young men watch with desire trying to hide their desire from each other – it is improper . . . she will either be his wife or his friend's . . . in either case signs of lust, of desire, are improper. She will belong to one of them. It is a curse on the one who owns her knowing everyone wants her and makes her his own in his bed, and a curse on those who will never touch her, who will not feel the warmth of her skin, her tender breasts on their lips, her hips against the fire of their loins. Oh, Emine! Emine! She will choose someone.

They line up in the small yard in the village of Aksaray, in the province of Konya in mid-Anatolia. The sun is setting, the earth is copper, it is bathed in the blood rays of the sun. The last flames linger on the *kerpiç* walls. The rays catch the straw gold strands enmeshed in the brown soil bricks used to build the houses. Fires have been lit. Food is being cooked in large pots. Everyone is invited, everyone comes, it is a moment of communal joy.

It is the women's turn to dance, the men have lined up in the yard. Emine's sister is beautiful and barely sixteen, her father reluctant to give her away. He can't according to custom, anyway; she would bring bad luck if he married her off before her older sister. She would bring bad luck on her sister as she would not find anyone to marry her, and bad luck on the whole household. Probably a tradition set by the elders to ensure that the older, less fortunate daughter is not robbed of marriage and stays at home all her life. Now it has become a semi-religious state of bringing a curse on to a household . . . bad luck! Now Emine, brown-eyed, olive-skinned, heart-shattering smile, Emine can marry. She could choose the best in the village. Not only this village – any of the villages around for miles. Just anyone. Just anyone her heart desires. And her father loved her. Loved her to death. He didn't see anyone but her. Even his son was not as important to him as Emine. She could have anyone her heart desired. He had prepared her dowry. He had the plot of land and house ready for her. On her wedding he would give her the fertile lands down by the river bed. Emine, the light of his eyes!

'You whore! What time do you call this? Tell me, you fuck-ing bitch! Where have you been?'

'I was at . . .' she says with a quiet voice. She is scared. She tries to shuffle sideways through the door.

'Come here! I told you to come here!' he roars. She doesn't move. She stands by the door as though nailed to the floor.

'Come here, I tell you!' pointing his fingers to a space by his feet. Spit splutters from his mouth, his eyes venomous, his neck red, muscles tense,veins standing up. The children are becoming uneasy, confused. They begin to whimper. She feels if this goes on they will begin to howl and scream uncontrollably. One is in the pram, the other holding on to the pram. She looks up at her mum, then at her father. She seeks comfort where there isn't any. Emine tries to touch the little girl's shoulder, her hand moves to her hand on the pram, she feels her own hand nervous, shaking. The girl is no more than four. She senses the fear and violence in the air. She moves from one foot to the other, watching her father and mother. The mother stands still, trying not to show her fear, feeling the little girl watching her.

'Don't shout in front of the children,' she manages to say, trying not to make it offensive.

'In front of the children!' comes the mocking roar, 'I'll give you in front of the children!' He moves towards her in long strides and grabs her by the collar. 'It's OK when you fuck in front of your children! When you are a whore! When I ask you a question who are you to tell me not to shout! What right do you have to ask me that question! Is that what you want? You want me to be quiet? All right . . . Where have you been till this time of night, you whore? Huh? Where have you been? Is this quiet enough? Is this all right then? Eh?' His face almost touching hers as he hisses. And suddenly he lets go of her dress, crumpled in his fist, and hits her face. Her hair goes flying, she holds her head in place. The side of her face is burning. She feels a fist coming down on her head like a hammer.

She is aware of her daughter running away and scream-ing. The little boy in the pram has been jolted, the shouting has woken him up. He looks bewildered, his eyes follow the movement of legs around him. The little girl has run away to the settee. She looks at her father with large frightened eyes. She watches very carefully.

'I am listening . . . where were you? Yes? I can't hear you!' He mockingly pushes his ear forward with the cup of his hand and leaning over her. She tries to protect her head with her arms. She uses the pram as a shield against him. She tries to squeeze herself into the corner of the room.

'I can't hear you . . . you daughter of a whore! Where have you been whoring?' He hits her repeatedly on the shoulders and head with his fist. He moves to the side of the pram and kicks her legs.

'No wife of mine can come home this late at night. This is not a whorehouse. This is a respectable house. Do you hear me? Do you?' He leans over to her ear and shouts with rage. He hits her again. 'Do you hear me? I am not a pimp and this is not a whorehouse. Don't come back here again. You think you can walk the streets on your own? You think you can walk the streets of Stoke Newington on your own, down Green Lanes, past all those cafés and all those people know you are my wife? Alone this time of night, you whore? I won't be able to show my face around the cafés because of you. They'll laugh and say, your wife was on her own, Kemal, I saw her at midnight last night walking down Green Lanes on her own. So what was she doing on her own at that time of night in the middle of Newington Green? Where was she coming from, then? You whore . . . you make my reputation shit . . . not worth tuppence!'

She slowly looks up as he has stopped hitting her. 'You should stand up to them. You know where I was. You know I was coming from the women's centre. We had a meeting. We had a meeting with a councillor. I wasn't whoring around.' Before she could finish she saw him turn around and hit her with his fist. He caught the side of her upper lip. Blood started flowing from her mouth. She could hear her daughter crying.

'I will shut that mouth of yours . . . I will shut it for you for good. You think you are clever, don't you . . . you think you are clever. You think no one can shut your mouth for you. Your father didn't teach you manners, did he? You talked back, didn't you? But I will teach you to shut your mouth. What the fuck do I care about the councillor! You are my wife. Your place is in this house. Looking after me, my children, my house, my business. You have no business going out at night and walking down Green Lanes where everyone can see you and call me a pimp! Do you get that? Do you?'

He leaned over her and grabbed her by the hair. He banged her head against the wall. She screamed as the side of her face felt the whole impact of the wall. She felt a sharp pain against her high cheekbone. She held her head, trying to pull her hair away from his grip, trying to loosen it so it didn't hurt so much as he pulled. She began to cry and spit blood over him. She wanted him to be covered with her blood. She tried to hit him at the same time, trying to defend herself. Her two small hands were delivering some blows wherever they landed. She wiped the blood from her mouth and tried to smear his face, his arms, his white shirt with it, all the time thinking she had to wash it. She was angry. He moved away. She moved towards him in her fury, 'You bastard! It's easy to hit me, isn't it. Yes go on, go on, hit me . . . you are so fucking brave, aren't you? Oh, so brave! Just because your friend says you are a pimp . . . hit me! That's how big a man you are! Oh, yes! You are such a man . . . all you can do is hit me!'

The front of her dress was covered in blood, her mouth, her teeth were covered in blood. She tried to stop it, felt her teeth to see if any were loosened by the blow. They were solid. She was relieved. She spat on the floor, tears rolling down her eyes, screaming and screaming at him now that she had found a voice to scream. She couldn't care that both her children were also screaming with her. She couldn't control it any more, she screamed almost hysterically. Through her tears she noticed that he had moved away from her, she noticed the blood stains on the carpet where she spat, she couldn't help thinking she had to clean it tomorrow. He had moved away now, slightly worried by the sight of blood. She screamed in anger, in frustration at her own impotence, just screaming and screaming as though she was a young girl.

During a lull she heard her children screaming and stopped. She listened to them and their sobs. She sat on the floor, just listening, unable to pick them up to hug them, to comfort them. She wanted someone to hug her, to comfort her. She slowly moved and tried to get up, numbed. She went into the bathroom to clean herself up and get ready to prepare dinner as she heard him shut the front door on his way out.

'This woman's project is important to us. It's our life-line!' says Emine with her son on her lap. She is holding a bottle to his mouth, one arm under his head. She is agitated. She looks at the councillor from Islington Council who has come to Newington Green to talk to them.

'You can't shut our project down! We built it. We worked for it. A whole generation of women have given their life for this project. We had to face assaults, beatings, abuse, harassment from husbands, fathers, brothers . . . a whole lot of opposition, let alone the crap we had to face from racists and men in British society. What are you talking about? You don't even know the meaning of the word to face all this and still carry on . . .'

The interpreter interprets what Emine is saying. The councillor looks at her and makes a movement with her hand, indicating she understands. 'Yes, but . . . because of the council tax and government spending cuts we can't afford to fund these projects any more,' she says.

The interpreter has difficulties trying to translate the intricacies of council tax and government spending arrangements with local councils. She finds a way of fudging it. The women are not interested. Emine is not interested.

'You spend thousands on useless projects, throw away thousands. We've had this project for ten years . . . ten years. No one did anything for us except these women around this project. You've never done anything for us . . . for us Turkish, Kurdish and Cypriotturkish women in this council. Show me what you've done. We did it all. Women before us did it. We forced you to employ Turkish-speaking council officers. You sat around on your backsides telling us there were no qualified experienced people for the jobs. If it was left to you, you would have never found anyone. We set up this project, we gave a chance to young women to train, to gain experience, a chance for abused women, deserted women, single parents, some subjected to violence by husbands, so that we could keep this project open. We gave women a chance, we gave each other a chance. You took some of the women we trained and even some of those have forgotten on whose backs they got jobs. Some don't even come near our projects now . . . they walk around with their noses in the air saying they are professionals or they don't want to be mixed up in all this. Well yes . . . they have to protect their jobs and we have learned to deal with those who have sold out. But this project is all we have and you can't shut down this lifeline we have. You have no right!' Emine was getting agitated, moving to the edge of her seat as she was talking, gesticulating in her excitement, her hand holding the *yemeni* she had swiped off her head with a quick movement. Her son was bouncing, still asleep, from one leg to the other in her lap, while she was folding first one leg then the other under her.

'Emine is right! You didn't set this project up. Other Turkish-speaking women before us did. They worked for nothing. You think it's easy to set up a project? And especially for Turkish-speaking women? Do you know what we suffer? Do you? And do you care?' Aysel jumped in, she couldn't control herself any more. She was a mother of four and a machinist at home.

'Yes, but the council tax . . . this government has attacked . . .'

'We don't want to hear about the council tax!' Fatma said.

'Not the council tax again!' said Hatice.

'We don't want to hear about the tax, Mrs Councillor! All we care about is our project. And, anyway, we pay our tax!'

This grabbed the imagination of the women crammed into a tiny room in an office in Newington Green.

'We pay our tax! And we are Islington residents. What have you done for us? And we paid our rates before then for years and what have you done for us? You come here to patronise us?'

'They are right!' A well-spoken woman with long black hair sitting among the women looked at the councillor and with self-assurance continued, 'You continuously try to patronise us. You play games to mystify situations to make it confusing for us . . . as though we don't understand what goes on. You try to camouflage your racism and your tokenism. You think that women are a soft option. You think that women who are not able to articulate their needs and aspirations, especially black and bilingual women, you think are a pushover.

'You are not even aware of the struggle women have to put up just to attend this centre. Do you know of the violence, the opposition they have to put up with just to come here? Do you know of the isolation they suffer? The racism they face in the streets, in the hospitals when they have to go for check-ups, when they take their children to the school gates, the name-calling and racism they face in the streets around here? Do you know of the aggravation and at times the violence they have to put up with in their homes from their husbands just so they can come out for a few hours each week to breathe, to talk, to share, to learn?

'You don't! How could you? You're a white middle-class woman living in Islington. You don't have to bring your washing in and wash it again because it has been smeared with shit. I could use the word excrement for sensitive ears but why should I spare you the brutality of it? You don't have to live in fear waiting for a brick to come through your window or a petrol bomb through your letter box, you don't have to live in fear of your husband being picked up by the police who have swooped on a café in Hackney or Islington or on one of the sweat shops, you don't have to cry after someone in your family who has been deported. No, you don't have to suffer any of this, do you? There's no family around here who does not face humiliation, harassment or deportation on a daily basis . . . or even attacks in the streets.

'As women, as Turkish-speaking women, we act like sponges, we absorb all the anger of our husbands, our children, our sons and daughters . . . we become the target of frustration and humiliation that our families suffer at work, in the streets, at school, in the factories, in official places. Women suffer all this . . . and we set up a project for ourselves to try and lessen this burden, to try and prevent ourselves from going mad, to try and share our pain and suffering and find some strength in ourselves, you try and shut our project down and throw us out of these miserable premises, out on the streets.

'You are not doing us any favours! We have a right to services which you don't make accessible to us and a right to set up this self-help group. What you need to do is to listen to what we are saying. Stop this tokenistic and openly racist position against us. We have every right to be here and have our project funded. We have already paid for that project in our taxes and our families have paid for it in colonial history, you are not giving us anything for nothing. It is ours by right!'

She was angry, her large brown eyes betrayed her anger, but she spoke with eloquence, without missing a beat in the rhythm of her speech. The women clapped noisily when she finished, laughed and shouted. *'Yaşa abla!'* shouted Emine, waving her *yemeni*. They all knew she would do a good job of it. Some knew her from the old days, others had heard of her. She was the founder of the project many years ago. Although she had moved to another part of London and was setting up other projects, she still came when they needed her.

Mrs Councillor looked a little embarrassed. She had nothing to say. All her arguments were tackled by the woman with the long hair. It would have been pointless trying to raise other objections or prolong the debate, the woman knew the system inside out and presented her arguments with admirable force. Eloquently and passionately. She had heard her before, she was known not only among the Turkish-speaking communities but also in other anti-racist and Black struggles. She commanded respect from all quarters. Sometimes fear, but respect all the same. She wished she had a few like her on her side. She thanked them and said she would do her best.

Emine pushes the pram through the door. Her face is lowered and her *yemeni* hangs over her forehead.

'*Hoşgeldin* Emine! Great to see you! Where have you been? We haven't seen you for a few days. We thought you had forgotten us, that you weren't going to come!'

Emine pushes the pram in, concentrating on manoeuvring the wheels. They hear her say, 'No one can stop me from coming to this centre . . . no one!' She leans over and looks at her son in the pram. Aysel and Hatice go up to help her. They are happily joking and laughing outrageously. One picks up the son and starts making baby talk and hugging and kissing him, squashing his soft face against her dark skin. The other picks up the little girl and begins to take her coat off. It's early summer but it is cold. Tea is boiling, the double pot gives a slight sound which adds to a sense of security. Some women are sitting around the table talking, others are smoking. One of the advisers is sticking new notices up, pulling old ones down. 'Don't forget about it, will you? We have a conference on Sunday. We are going to talk about lots of things,' she says.

'What are we going to talk about, Gonce?'

'Health, breast and cervical cancer . . .'

'What about virginity?'

'If you want to . . . and work. Different careers open to women. How you could progress, do something different in life. About racism and how it affects us. How we can increase our confidence in challenging it. That sort of thing.'

'What about violence? Violence against women by their husbands?' says Emine.

'We all have that dear, dear Emine . . .' says Aysel, laughing. 'You know what they say in our community: *Dayak Cennetten çıktı*, beatings are from Heaven.' She turns to face Emine, who had stood up, and nearly drops the baby when she sees Emine's blood-covered broken swollen lip, her black eye, and the distorted side of her face – bruised blood clots and the skin grazed off.

running hot

DREDA SAY MITCHELL

MEHMET ALI lay in East London's number one outdoor spot to die. He lay two doors down from Kwame's Hotshot barbers and three doors up from Roseman's cabs. Over him rocked the bodies of two men as they stomped, twisted and sliced their shoe heels into him. An hour earlier his attackers had been jerking their bodies to the pounding energy of Judge Dredd's Nightsound. Now they continued their dance by fucking him up. At first their movements had been light, verbal in nature, with the need to find what they were after. But their tactics had changed once they realised his lips weren't moving. After they had found him, like they knew they would, they'd dragged him to Cinnamon Junction, right on to the main road. They had known that this spot was too notorious, too in your face, for any of the cars passing at 2.23 a.m. to stop and help. Anyway, any car cruising the Junction at that time of morning had its own business to attend to.

Benji, the more bullish of the two, stopped, tipped back on to the wall and breathed, allowing the greatness of power to balloon within his body. His gloved hand grabbed the forearm of his partner.

'We'd better stop and find it . . .'

'Whatever,' Josh responded, his body spinning on too much booze and barbs.

'Let's see if the fool's hurting enough to spill,' Benji continued loudly, wanting their victim to understand the next move.

So they demanded from him. Yelled at him. Shook him so many different ways that the only music serenading the new day was the cooing pain from Mehmet's throat. But their dance had been too synchronised, too perfect in its damage as he only heard the blood draining and drying around his ears. They demanded from him one last time. He wasn't giving it up and they knew it. Frustration intensified their blows. In the middle of a slanted heel movement, Benji wobbled as his head snaked towards the road.

'I can hear Blue Bottles,' he whispered, as his shoe meshed with bone.

'I can't hear a thing,' Josh answered, slowing his attack.

'Let's settle for ten,' Benji continued, 'and then check back, because let me tell you, if we don't find the t'ing – this'll be us soon enough.'

As they scattered, their victim had already decided he would never tell them. Better to be dead at the Junction than at the hands of his own people. He used his shoes to scrape into the pavement and push himself back and away from the road, needing to get back the merchandise he had flicked when he realised he was being followed.

Mehmet Ali died at 2.31 a.m., just as the last anonymous car had blown by, throwing a Tennant's can from its window, which rolled like the softest lullaby on his still stomach.

Schoolboy, known to the criminal justice system as Elijah Ray Campbell, stepped off the N66 bus as it hit the Junction and hit 2.33 a.m. He stretched his legs as a police car screamed past carrying its hysteria long into the distance. The bus bolted as he eased into air consumed with the fumes of throwaway food. He shuffled back from the peeling metal rail that guarded the pavement from the road, needing to sort out his thoughts. Only a few people realised that 2.30 to 3 was the Junction's serene zone. No people. No aggravations. No unexpected moments. The ideal place to think. Also he knew that most would wrongly mark him as a crackhead too worthless to trouble, too useless to know better than to flaunt himself there at that time of the morning. His eyes grinned with remembered freedom at discovering this time.

His eyes shut down as the weathered stench of one too many slashes against the wall streamed by. Nothing like touching other people's lives to spoil a pure moment. He slipped sideways as he reached The Raven, a club that beat out a rapid 'come and check me' pulse and stood so dark in its skin of black paint that night-dwellers were either enticed into going inside or taking up its offer of using its street shadows to hide in. Schoolboy slid into its shadow. He re-focused. He'd already made his decision. He was going whether anyone liked it or not. They would expect to see him at the start of next week and they wanted commitment – bottom line. He could get down with that. They had been ultra clear that commitment meant bringing his own knives. Knives he didn't have. Being a Giro-slave and making a few bad turns in his last skimming enterprise meant he had no silver to spare. He dismissed doing a residential or a commercial. That part of his life was done. He took a breath. Deep. He was going and if that meant finding a good home for the loose change of his nearest and dearest, then so be it. He needed to gather the cash quickly as by Sunday he would be on West Coast Mainline headed for Devon. He shook his head. He still couldn't believe it – bloody Devon, the type of place where those that thought they were in the know would assume his middle name was either Winston or Delroy. But it would be worth it. It had to be worth it.

As the voices of the passing car engines scatted high and low, Schoolboy began running through schemes and names which could get the knife relief fund started. Option one was Terri-baby, his current. She'd do anything for him. Well, nearly anything. But he was too fucked off with her. Too fucked that Little-Miss-Middle-Class-Self didn't think he was good enough to meet Daddy and Step Mommy. Good enough to shag on their sofa though. Option two was Emmanuel, who had been his main spar. The only trouble was four months ago Manny had become Mr Ten Days Church of the Living Lord, standing on the corner of Dalston Lane and Kingsland Road pleading with the pun-ters at Ridley Road market to get into the rhythm of the resurrection. Which left Evie. Option number three. Evie his up-and-coming sister. He knitted his fingers through his dreads, massaging his scalp, needing to get his story straight. Evie wasn't stupid. She knew the street, but every now and again her chosen life made her forget. Made her so radical she wanted to help people like him. He spat a large gob on to the pavement. She was so full of piss sometimes.

His whole head whipped away from the melting spittle as his stare fixed on to what looked like the upward palm of a naked foot and accompanying leg, the only visible sign of a body sandwiched in the gap between The Raven and the neighbouring building. He moved around and forward knowing it wasn't a Raven resident, as anyone and everyone knew The Raven took care of its own within its walls. He wasn't shocked. This end of the Junction was the most popular for advertising new brands of killing. The Junction was angry and it didn't care who knew it. Even the Blue Bottles understood this and buzzed right by it. Its anger had become so biting and bold that it was the one pitch in Hackney where the community passed through or around. They used it to move quickly from Hackney to Islington. Islington to Hackney. From living to dying. He returned his attention to the leg. It was covered in the same make of stepping-out trousers he had himself bought last week. Same flair. Same style. Sharp with the tailored swing of someone ready to move on. Shame they were spoiled by the wayward pattern of blood.

He moved his vision to the side, not willing to move it up, more comfortable looking at the collection of sagging bin bags. He followed their defeated shapes around until he unexpectedly stopped when he noticed a shoe. Right or left, he couldn't tell. It pointed at him, lying on its side, the space left for the placement of a foot, wide open, staring at him with the helplessness of a permanent scream. He moved towards it knowing someone else would have missed it. But not him. Since the age of thirteen he had trained his eyes to observe, catch everything, because he never knew when he might need something. Never knew when he might need to hold something in someone's face, just as a reminder.

The shoe's very poise and look made him uncomfortable. He had enough grief in his life without some shoe thinking it could join the flippin' queue. He booted it backwards, scattering glass from the broken street lamp and revealing an object that resembled a half brick. He stilled himself, knowing he shouldn't get involved. Only seven more days to keep his fingernails clean. But when opportunity has been the most influential instigator in helping to decide which corner to turn, it wasn't that easy. He folded his legs at the knees, scooped it up, already having identified it as a mobile. It was a relic. The type of mouthpiece the average street thief would give back to his victim in disgust. If you can't insure it, don't nick it. He wiped the watery dirt from its backside and rationalised that he could leave it, but someone out there might already be collecting this type of dinosaur to add to tomorrow's list of antiques. Option number four took hold and began to tell its own story – sell mobile and SIM card as a package for fifty quid to Mikey and fleece Evie for another thirty. That way he could purchase at least one blade and also some fine home-grown Amsterdam he'd heard was doing revolutionary mouth-to-mouth resus. Nothing like leaving London with the aroma of something special flossing his teeth. Decision made, he forced the mobile into the pocket of his fleece.

As he began heading for the traffic lights at the end of the Junction, he knew he should be feeling guilty – stealing from the dead and all that, but the man didn't need it where he was going. Going? The Brother was undoubtedly already gone. But whether he was smoked or just well-done was none of Schoolboy's business. Now he needed to decide who he would go to first. Mikey or Evie? Evie or Mikey? Mikey would be easy, just a simple business transaction. Goods for money. Now Evie would be harder. She could easily afford thirty sovs but she wouldn't want to give it up. At least not without running her mouth all over him for a minimum of half an hour.

Abruptly, one of those unexpected moments crashed into his stride and he was shaken. Shaken by the sight of two men coming his way. Shaken, because maybe he didn't know the Junction as well as he should. His shock let go as he marked them for what they were – a pair of freelance amateurs. Classic asylum-seekers, if he was correct, trying to plant new soil in the capital. Only amateurs masqueraded in lengthy leather coats, unbuttoned to create flow and drama as they proceeded down the street. The only drama they played out was pure shaft. Pure panto. London's freelancers were now marketing themselves as consultants, all tooled-up in cottons and linen.

But Schoolboy recognised that even amateurs knew how to use a 9mm or create some other type of life-altering moment. As he passed them he cast his eyes downwards, letting them have their illusion of fear and respect. He'd also long ago realised that if someone didn't catch a glimpse of your eyes or stare directly into them, they were unlikely to remember your face. He didn't look back. 'Keep your face forward' were the last words his Mum had sternly soothed him with before she'd boarded the plane back home to Grenada. And he did just that, until his gates came into view.

Schoolboy was long gone before they realised they wouldn't find the phone. Long gone before they realised that they might have been ripped off. Long gone before they realised the only street parasite they had seen had passed them a good ten minutes ago. They tipped out the word on to Hackney's major highways to find him.

like a road

STEF PIXNER

NANA ALWAYS ASKED, got a boyfriend, then? And Sammy always said, no Nana, you know me, I'm too busy. And she is too busy, much too busy for Ed, who is always round these days, insinuating himself into her life like honey into hot toast, mixing their photos up together when she likes them in separate albums, mixing up their books and CDs. He even wants to meet Sammy's Nan.

Sammy decided, a long time ago when she was sixteen, that she would never ever take another boyfriend to meet her Nan. She'd done it once, and that was enough. Nana had a shrivelling look when she disapproved of something or someone. It could be set off by bits of fluff on your clothes, but boyfriends were the surest trigger. Nobody's boyfriend or husband was any good. Sammy hadn't even told her Nan she'd got married, the two times she'd got as far as the registry office. Sammy is now twenty-seven and Nana is, as far as Sammy knows, still waiting for the wedding.

Ed has been around a few months and it's getting to be time things went one way or the other. Some men drape themselves across Sammy like she's a washing line; she carries them for a while, and then the line breaks. Ed's quiet, but she likes the way he dunks his head in the bathwater, shakes it dry and reaches out for the soap with his eyes still shut.

Nana is in her nineties now. Sammy hasn't seen her for two years. It's not just the long journey that puts her off, or the fact that you can't be sure Nana will be in once you get there because she can't hear the phone any more, or remember which hour is which. It might help if Sammy could drive. But something else stops her from going, even though Sammy and her sister used to spend weeks with Nana as children and Sammy thinks about her Nan almost every day.

Pretend you're a solicitor, Sammy says to Ed as his car stalls on top of the hill above her Nan's. Ed is in the passenger seat next to her despite the promise he'd gone on about never to teach another girlfriend to drive. Pretend you've got a job with good prospects, says Sammy. Switch the engine on again, says Ed.

The hill drops away so breathtakingly you'd think the car might fly. Far below them you can see Nana's house, tucked between the railway, the gasworks and the dual carriageway, one little matchbox in a thin joined-up row. Nana will have changed, that's for sure. A bag of skin and bones might answer the door, or it won't open at all, and a smell of death will come wafting through the letterbox. They want you to move off, says Ed.

One of the things about Sammy's driving is she gives way to every car on the road. She is now giving way to the cars behind her. They are objecting loudly to the courtesy, and the jarring sound of horns from the tailback on the hill is making her panic. Everything goes liquid when Sammy's behind the wheel, and liquid pours off her too. Switch the engine on again, says Ed.

Sammy looks in her rearview mirror and catches a sideways view of him. What will her Nan think of the ring through Ed's eyebrow, and his glittering studded nose? Or the way he's shaved his head up the sides and left his bleached blonde hair sticking up in the middle like a new bath brush? Don't listen to those creeps, says Ed. Just move off in first.

What Nana won't know is Ed has more piercings than you'd think, in places you wouldn't expect and Nana wouldn't approve of. When Sammy first had her ears pierced, Nana gave her The Look. You're like a savage, she said, that's just come from the jungle. What's wrong with savages, said Sammy, who always argued with her Nan. But Nana knew for certain what beauty was, and she knew for sure it would bring happiness – even though Nana had been beautiful once herself, and Sammy had never seen her happy. In fact her Nan is just about the unhappiest person Sammy has ever come across, and it's all because of losing her baby and Grandpa all in one go. Grandpa went off with a dental assistant soon after their six-month-old baby Owen died of pneumonia, and that's when, according to Sammy's aunt, Nana began dressing up in her best whenever she went to the bus stop, or to sit on a bench in the park.

Sammy isn't sure about Ed's piercings, either. Not the ones below the waistline, anyway. Belly button not too bad, but scrotum, I ask you. He keeps coming back with more of them, like the one on his chin. And that's not all he collects. Sammy noticed yet another toothbrush stuck in the mug this morning when she was wiping his shaving foam off the mirror. Then he appeared in the mirror beside her, lanky and handsome, with his collapsible look, like a deckchair or a camel. Let the clutch up slowly, says Ed. He puts his hand on Sammy's on the gearstick and warmth spreads up her arm.

Nana and Sammy used to stand for hours in front of the mirror, looking at themselves, holding hands. Sammy would smile up at Nana, and Nana would smile into the mirror for the Prince she was expecting – preferably a doctor or a lawyer. She would be wearing a dark red dress with buttons down the front. Dark red was Nana's favourite colour, and she loved buttons. Silver buttons, pearly buttons, buttons the exact shade of the cloth – or, most subtle and stylish of all, buttons covered with the self-same fabric, done by a dressmaker who came to the house. Nana would touch her freshly done jet-black hair, and coax its curls. Leave the handbrake till you're ready to move off, says Ed.

The privet at the end of Nana's once neat front garden has arched over the gate and met at the top. The thin garden has run wild. Brambles crawl across the path. Weeds have choked the mint where Sammy's tortoise used to dream of racing hares. We won't stay long, says Sammy, about to bang on the door, we'll just have a cup of tea and then go. I don't mind how long we stay, says Ed. I do, says Sammy. I mind a lot. Bang bang. No movement inside the house. Bang bang bang. Silence. Sammy doesn't dare lift up the letterbox. Let's try round the back, says Ed.

On the back wall of the house the pebbledash is missing most of its pebbles up to child height. There's a french door, and a window either side of it. The curtains are closed. Look through the gap, says Ed. Sammy climbs the step up to the french door and peers through a crack between the curtains. It's too dark in the room to see anything. She knocks on the glass and stands back. Nothing. Let's go, Ed, says Sammy. Try again, says Ed. Sammy knocks and knocks, and then the curtains flicker.

A puzzled face appears at the window. The three of them watch each other, Nana as still as an animal surprised by a predator, before recognition hits and her face is transformed with joy. She rattles at the door handle, several times, then disappears. She is gone for a long time. Sammy hears a train from behind them; the railway is just across the unmade road at the back. What was once a lullaby is now a high-speed intercity whoosh. She used to sleep well at her Nan's, trains rattling their long-distance rhythms, like she sleeps well with Ed when he curls round her at night, his breath coming and going on the back of her neck. Where can Nana have got to? She must have forgotten they're there.

But here's Nana at last, with a large pair of dressmakers' scissors held high, a toothless grin of pure delight that Sammy has never seen on her Nan's face before – and her covered buttons undone to the waist to reveal long hanging breasts that are likewise new for Sammy. At the sight of them Sammy gets a sharp pain in her chest. But Nana waves the scissors gaily at her and Ed, then bends and tries to cut the tangle of knots she has tied from the door handle to the window catch. She bends for a long time, her white head bobbing. Then at last it's done, the door's open and they're in.

The whole house stinks, like a fox's hole or the rodent house at the zoo.

Nana is very bent. Her hands are shiny and her fingers bulbous. Her hair is white and straight and long, with jet black tips.

We've just dropped in for a cup of tea, says Sammy, glancing at her Nana before making straight for the gas stove in the kitchen, wanting something normal or practical to do: I'll make it. But the gas stove isn't normal any more. Or practical. Nana! What's happened to the gas stove? Where are the bits that go on top? All Sammy can see is the pipes that feed the gas jets, the ones usually hidden under a white enamel plate. Nana looks sly. She's dismantling her life, says Ed who is fingering the silver stud on his chin. How would you know? says Sammy, but Nana takes Ed by the hand into the back room as if she's known him for years. Clearly Ed has made a hit with Sammy's Nan. Sammy begins to look for the missing gas stove parts.

Nana hasn't just taken the stove apart, she's hidden the bits. Perhaps a person gets tired of cooking, after seventy years of it, though Nana's cooking was always good, with loads of butter and the lightest pastry. Sammy looks under the table and in the cupboard under the stairs. She looks under the sofa in the front room, and behind the small chest of drawers in the hall. It's not just the stove Nana's dismantled. She's taken down photos from the mantelpiece and pictures from the walls, and it's unsettling, with all those pale empty squares looking at Sammy out of the dust, as if life is like a road you walk on that you can roll up behind you as you go.

But Nana hasn't rolled up everything. Upstairs is very different from the neat and tidy bedrooms Sammy and her sister used to sleep in. It looks like Nana has shaken the contents of her drawers out over the floors, and then stirred them up. There is a sea of heaps. Sammy keeps coming across cheerful postcards from herself, from all parts of the globe. Nana seems to have kept everything, though she always complained when other people did. She went further than just complaining. She once went through Sammy's drawers when Sammy was in the other room, and threw out her letters into Next Door's garden. The first Sammy knew about it was when Next Door rang the bell and said, Use your own f-word dustbin.

There are also heaps of unsent or first draft letters from Nana to other people. For example, a note addressed to the proprietor of Sea View Guest House, Abbey Sands, dated soon before Sammy was born, which says, *Please keep an eye on my daughter, the man she has just married is a maniac* – which could be why Sammy's parents always gave Nana a wide berth. Or the letter underneath it on the pile (which Sammy already knows about), written the week Sammy's sister gave birth to a dead baby, which says, *You couldn't even look after a kitten*.

Sammy goes into her old bedroom, which faces the back. Nana has taken the ornaments off the mantelpiece – the sailor doll and the Chinese dragon teapot, and put them on the floor in front of the electric fire. There are more letters strewn about, some lying on the bed Sammy used to sleep in. They mostly seem to be to Sammy's aunts, complaining about their husbands. One husband is tied to his mother's apron strings, one smacks the children, the other is a van driver. There are others, scattered on the floor, addressed to *The Beast from Bolton. What a scrooge you are! What about that £11 fourteen and six? You squander money, but only on yourself! You were a gentleman before we were married, of course. Before that nasty mother of yours came over the Baltic for the wedding and never went back!*

Sammy kicks at a pile of letters and hears a ring of metal. One of the gridirons. The kick has also dislodged some familiar photos that used to be on the mantelpiece. Nana has cut them into pieces. Here's a picture of Sammy with her hands cut off. And a fat beaming baby Owen cut through the eye. Sammy urgently wants to make the tea and go.

Sammy's sister refused to see Nana after she lost the baby, and has never seen her since. You'd think she'd know how it felt, she said. Nana lost a baby too.

Sammy feels sick and goes to the bathroom. Her period is three weeks late. Tears roll down her cheeks like big globs of egg white. Sometimes she dreams of babies who are lost and cold and can't get home. Three of the chrome rings that go round the gas jets turn up in the laundry basket, and under them, her fingers find what turns out to be a letter to Sammy herself. *Of course you can't spare **one** (underlined three times) hour in your busy schedule to see **me**. I haven't spoken to **anyone** for **three days**.* Sammy sits down on the bathroom floor. She looks at the now unevenly pink paint which Nana has tried cleaning up to her shoulder height, the pink bath veiled with lime-scale, the laminated plastic poem on the wall: *Please remember, don't forget! Never leave the bathroom wet!*

She can hear shouting from outside. Sammy gets up and goes to look out of her old bedroom window. Ed is underneath it with a bucket and cloth. Busybody! shouts Nana. If I want to see I go outside! If I want to see I go to the shops! I don't go to other people's houses and start washing their windows! I don't interfere in other people's houses! You can help me, says Ed, putting a cloth in her hand.

After twenty minutes Sammy finds the second gridiron under a wardrobe along with a crumpled envelope with her name on it. Inside the envelope, and dated a couple of months ago, Nana has written a note in red biro which says, *Thank you for your nice postcard from Peru.* On the back of it she has scrawled, *Sammy, you're my baby now.*

Sammy was in Peru five years ago. Perhaps Nana, coming across the card again recently, thought it had only just arrived. Sammy smiles. This must be the first time Sammy's Nan has ever thanked her for anything.

Sammy goes downstairs and fits the parts she's found on top of the stove. She's got everything now except for the flame spreaders. In the back room, the TV is crackling. Where have you hidden the flame spreaders, Nana? Are they in here? But Nana and Ed, having finished with the windows, are now busy with the TV. It is bright with zigzags and wavy lines. At last a picture appears with some heads at the bottom of the screen and some feet at the top. Nana is delighted, but Ed starts fiddling with the knobs at the back, his arm stretched round the TV, his face peering at the screen. Nana puts her arm round the other side of the TV to reach the knobs herself. She's holding my hand, says Ed, smiling at Sammy. Sammy notices that when Ed smiles, the ring in his eyebrow lifts up. And so does something in Sammy's chest.

Sammy looks under cushions, in the waste basket, behind the divan. Maybe you can boil a kettle without flame spreaders? Back in the kitchen she lights the gas and a two foot blue flame shoots up like a laser beam. You can't boil a kettle on that, says Nana, peremptory, shuffling into the kitchen. Although she has shrunk, Nana's nostrils seem to have got larger. Large, and red inside. Nana takes a teapot from the dresser. Very very slowly. Her hands are trembling. She puts three spoons of tea in the pot, adds cold water from the tap, and puts it on the shelf above the electric fire in the back room.

Sammy finds cups, saucers, a tin of evaporated milk, a sugar bowl, a tea cosy, a hand-embroidered tablecloth from

China, a packet of crispbread and some cherry jam. Once she made pretend tea for her Nan from mud water, and Nana drank it from pretend cups. Now Sammy will make pretend tea again. It takes time to locate a tin opener, but at last there's milk in the bottom of the cups. Although she knows the tea water will never heat up, Sammy is going to wait as if it will.

Tea's ready, she calls after the right amount of time has gone by. There is laughter from the front room.

Meet my new girlfriend, says Ed, his arm round Nana. Nana giggles. All that waiting, and now her Prince has come.

the man who lived
on the train

KATHARINA RIST

IN THE RUSH OF THE HOUR Virginia hadn't been able to reserve a seat, so she installed herself in the mother and child compartment. The inspector would not be able to prove that she wasn't pregnant.

Opposite Virginia sat a small elderly man with sunglasses, who wore loose travel trousers and what appeared to be several jumpers one on top of the other. He was visibly pleased to have Virginia's company, lifted his glasses, stood up and introduced himself:

'Welcome to the train! You are the first traveller for months who has taken a place opposite me with an open expression. You have the face of a German Madonna, but that hardly detracts from your charm. The roguish features around your mouth and your even more roguish hold-all – ' (he pointed at Virginia's untidy piece of luggage, the contents of which were easy to guess, because it was bursting out on all sides) ' – transcend your face in a colourful way. You are an artist and a collector, however, also a victim of persecution and life doesn't land into your lap lightly.'

Virginia nodded and pulled out her notebook.

The stranger carried on: 'I am Baldwin and have lived on the train for thirteen years. I moved in here because it's important for me to have a beginning and an end. We already have enough vertical connections, you know. However, horizontal ones cross through my life in a confusing manner and I decided to live on a straight line. Others decide to lead a life completely in verticality and join an order. However, I did not want to leave the horizontal completely. Therefore I made my decision in favour of the train.'

Virginia made notes, adding Baldwin to her collection while he continued:

'I like walking and soaking up light and air. This feels very good – here in the train. You don't get lost, you know the direction. I pass through both the train and the world as if I am wearing seven-league boots. Also, the characters keep changing. Some remain, others have left, newcomers have joined in. Some have grown older, especially those who have stayed outside for long. Others return at the end in order to die here. Many come for this reason; however, mostly they don't realise it.'

The sound of hasty footfalls interrupted Baldwin's monologue. 'The puppet-boy comes,' he whispered, closing his eyes. The inspector opened the door of the compartment and Virginia showed her ticket. The man didn't pay any attention to the sleeping person.

Self-important steps left the compartment.

Baldwin opened his eyes and continued: 'These fellows disturb the daily routine enormously. Puppet-boys, mastered by others. However, they impose a structure on the day, just as the announcements at the stations do. It is calming, if you know what is coming, and yet there are daily variations, for instance, when the name of the next station is being shouted out. Some voices proclaim the train's arrival ten minutes beforehand. This causes an immediate rummaging, digging and heaving and an outpouring of sometimes ten or twelve legs per compartment, who queue expectantly in front of the toilets, which makes me remain there for quite a time. However, this doesn't bother me any more. At nights I sleep there in a standing position. One should not forget about verticality. The toilets are also too tiny and dirty to make it cosy lying there. In earlier times I managed to do it diagonally, but it isn't pleasant to half fall down into the toilet itself, when the train stops sharply.'

'Are you not able to sleep in the compartment?' asked Virginia.

'You have to give the puppet-boys a feeling that you have a destination, that you get into the train and out, that you are busy and the train is only a transitory space. Commuters are fine, but people who never get out, that's impossible. Therefore you sometimes have to disappear. They are supposed to think you are someone else once they see you again. You wouldn't believe it, how stupid these fellows are.'

Virginia nodded, being experienced in grief.

'You can show some of these fellows just any piece of paper, and they punch it officiously, their faces overwhelmed with importance. Often they don't know where we come from and where we are going to. In particular, the inspectors of semi-fast trains know only their own tiny districts. When they have arrived at their border they return, as if the world was coming to an end, and then start at the beginning again. If passengers ask for information about stations which are outside their section, they look at them with faces like question marks, as if it is an insult to confront them with the world beyond their line. While other people start their lives in the past and conduct it teleologically into the future, these inspectors perform their lives in circles. Like migratory birds they go from A to B and return to A after a certain period of time. However, they don't go as far as these birds and therefore they think their section is the world. Hardly ever have I come across an inspector who wanted to know what was beyond his tiny final destination. Most of them are obsessed with the idea that they are doing something very good for humankind. They are supposed to catch people who try to avoid buying a ticket, aren't they? Listen to their voices and you know everything, Virginia. These people haven't made it outside the train. Often they are sent by psychiatrists. Their job is prescribed as occupational therapy and they even get money for it; and a blue cap, that's maybe the most important thing.'

Baldwin groped under his jumper and fished out an inspector's cap. 'I also have the other pieces of equipment in stock. Sometimes I need a bit of fun and to mingle with the puppet-boys. They never find out.'

'Of course not,' Virginia said, looking at his stomach which seemed to be some kind of Pandora's box. From under his jumper the old man brought out more and more objects into the daylight.

'Was there something that precipitated your final decision to move into the train, Baldwin?' asked Virginia.

Baldwin hesitated: 'Mmm. I usually prefer to give the philosophical reason only. Well . . . there was something else: in a way my wife sent me. She thought it was my only chance.'

Virginia couldn't believe her ears:

'How could she? Did she want to get rid of you? Did you betray her? Was she jealous?' Virginia overwhelmed him with questions. Baldwin struggled, before he came out with an answer: 'Not in the way you would assume. Jealousy, what is it? There was actually this big yellow ball crumpled in her mind poisoned with words, thoughts and actions which my internal policeman dared to disclose.'

'I beg your pardon?' Virginia asked, confused.

'Indeed, I had a policeman living in my heart. He completely filled it and had everything under control except on Fridays and Mondays, when he had his days off. It was on a Friday when I started to live in the train. I had to use my day off from him before he could change my mind again. I hurried up, packed my stuff and left in a rush. I was afraid that he might be able to follow me. This would have been my end. I left while he was having his breakfast. He always needed so many knives, forks and plates that I was able to disappear without him noticing me. He was so bloody accurate. Not only had he divided his life into squares but even the whole universe. There was not a single corner which wasn't named, numbered and fully assembled. My wife Olivia could not stand it. She went mad when we had to have sex between squares 561 and 562.'

Virginia looked at Baldwin in surprise. However, she thought that maybe it was better to have sex between squares 561 and 562 than have no sex at all.

Baldwin interrupted Virginia's train of thought by giving more details of his former life: 'The worst was when the imaginative queuing started. The policeman had decided it would help if we brought more order and discipline into our lives. We had to queue, even if no one was there. Whatever we did, we had to wait: even in front of our own bedroom. His mind was like a looking glass. If we didn't follow his rules and regulations he would mirror them into our brains until we couldn't do anything else but obey.'

'This sounds terrible,' Virginia commented.

Baldwin's face turned blank: 'The only way out was to

escape into a piece of limited moving space. My options, my visions, everything had to change into a measurable amount of space which couldn't be reached by him. So I left.'

Virginia enquired: 'What happened to your wife?'

Baldwin's voice trembled: 'I think she finally took the policeman as her husband replacement. He was in control of everything anyway, so she didn't need to do anything but queue. She seemed to be able to adapt to it in the end. However, she thought I would die if I didn't leave, and she was right.' Baldwin was quiet for a while, until Virginia became uncomfortable and felt the lack of conversation:

'Are you always here?' Virginia asked. She would have liked to bite her tongue off for the stupidity of the question.

'I am in all trains, you know. You have seen me before, but you were too busy collecting characters and didn't notice me.'

Virginia looked into her book with embarrassment while fidgeting with a pen.

'Thirteen years is a long time. Conductors come and go. Fashions change. New trains are being built. Once I only lived in slow trains. There was more space, and I was able to lay out the compartments according to my taste. I took all my living room furniture with me and spread plenty of boxes full of my things all over the train. The Intercity Express doesn't allow this kind of freedom any more. One is constantly bothered with disembodied voices coming out of the walls. However, eventually one stops needing so many objects. I am getting used to wearing most of the stuff on my body apart from some bulky items which I hide in secret places.'

Baldwin's speech was suddenly broken off by the door opening abruptly. A nervous mother heaved a pair of obese twins out of a push-chair. 'Are you travelling without any children in *this* compartment?' the woman asked accusingly. Baldwin didn't answer, fumbled under his jumper, stood up and left. Virginia had the impulse to follow him, but Baldwin gestured her to stay. He would return in time.

For Virginia a restless time began. Crying, breastfeeding, changing nappies. The little chaps didn't sleep at all but took turns in howling. The mother did nothing to stop them. 'When is *yours* due?' she asked instead, and looked at Virginia's belly in an impudent manner. 'Oh,' Virginia blushed. 'Not yet.' She would have to cut down her chocolate intake.

In Hanover mother and twins left. 'All the best for your child,' she shouted at Virginia, accompanying her remark with a smirk. The accused was angry: 'Luckily, it'll be a chocolate baby. Then I can always eat it up if it ever gets as horrible as your kids!' The twins' mother snorted, then she was gone.

Virginia's period of convalescence was short. Another mother got on the train. This one brought a five-year-old along who loudly and compulsively related every single thing he was thinking or doing. Simultaneously his fingers drummed on the window pane, as if they were independent beings detached from the body. For twenty minutes his mouth sang non-stop that he wanted to do poopoo and peepee. The louder the song, the stronger became the stench which emanated from his entire body – but his mother slept on. When his emanations began to stink out the whole compartment, Virginia lost her temper and woke the mother, who was furious. Virginia could have taken the child to the loo, couldn't she? The two disappeared towards the toilet.

Before the return of mother and child Virginia heard someone shuffling along the corridor. It was Baldwin. Virginia dragged him into the compartment, begging him to take action. Baldwin pulled a strange uniform from his repertoire and changed into something – but just what, Virginia was not able to work out straightaway. However, when mother and son, both stinking more than before, came back, Baldwin's body had actually spread over four seats. Head here, bottom there and other limbs lying scattered in confusion. In addition the old chap breathed stertorously, as if he was about to die any moment. Stinky farted in despair and made off, followed by his mother, screaming hysterically.

When the inspector arrived to sort out the trouble, everything was in perfect order. Baldwin was sitting there, a serious elderly gentleman with a monocle. The inspector apologised and left.

'Inside and outside are the same, Virginia,' Baldwin explained. 'At first, you don't realise – but after years you notice – that it doesn't matter whether we sit in front of the window pane or behind it. Having once been the border, the threshold, the separation between life in this world and the life hereafter, the pane eventually loses its function. The glass now connects rather than separates and invites us to look through it and cross over. We are not inside the vehicle while the people outside are pursuing their activities, but *they* are *inside* in the world, while *we* are *outside* and dwelling in a moving body. We are closer to the true being, because we have lost the ground under our feet. We are more like angels than humans.'

Virginia smiled. Baldwin looked like anything but an angel.

Baldwin fell silent until Kassel-Wilhelmshöhe. Shortly before the train stopped in Göttingen, he entered a dog-like sleep; and Virginia watched him, until he woke up in Frankfurt-am-Main. It was as if an imaginary figure had drawn a magic circle around the sleeping man, who filled the compartment with an aura that prevented other passengers from entering.

Virginia tried to do some writing. Images came and went; nothing happened but traces and cross-references. The compartment transformed more and more into a magical room, which excluded words and actions. So Virginia's thoughts wandered into a no man's land of wordless objects. Words were untied from language and strolled as geometrical figures silently through space. Virginia observed that the body of the elderly man was rocking jerkily backwards and forwards and that his upper ears pricked to each sound. Baldwin looked like an entwined figure who was giving birth to other shapes. Virginia had the feeling of growing older. Imagining a world without thresholds, Virginia noticed how Baldwin's body opened as if he entered the world while he slept and, vice versa, was able to let the world into his body.

Suddenly at Frankfurt Central station Baldwin rose from his sleep without any transition. Checking his monocle, he began:

'Once I was used to marching along quickly. Sometimes I jogged through the train, I rambled, strode and carried imaginary loads after me; I performed exercises, I sang, I slipped and I pranced. Nowadays each step counts. Stopping and shuffling balance one another. Walking has become more ponderous. More and more often I have to get out of the way. Voices I haven't summoned are invading from everywhere. They disturb my ways and thoughts.

Measuring steps out, shaping them meticulously, have become impossible. The steps are part of the language of this vehicle. This language is much more important than anything you might read here in the train, what is forced into your mind from everywhere. I would rather take to letterlessness. The Rushing, the *big rushing* has disappeared. The passengers don't know yet.'

'What rushing?' Virginia asked. 'Do you mean the rushing in the texts of the deconstructivists?'

Baldwin waved her words away. 'Why texts? For *the rushing* no texts are needed. The rushing is in us, inside me and outside of me – which means the same. You are very young, Virginia, very young. However, you will get older sooner than you think.'

Baldwin signalled a stop to any further communication, and when Virginia left the train in Freiburg, they parted without exchanging any words.

the iranian-american peanut butter goat cheese wrap

ANITA TADAYON

NAHAL WAS AN ONLY CHILD. Not really a significant fact, but it helps to give you context. Everyone has a context – their culture, their family, their school, and even their neighbourhood. If one of these elements of context were different, maybe Nahal would have a different story. Who knows? Nahal certainly wouldn't.

Nahal was a Tehrani, that is someone born in or living in Tehran. This meant her family were likely to be middle class in the Iranian society of the late 1970s. They had to be to afford to send her to Tehran's American Community School. Nahal had some idea of what it meant to be a Tehrani. She certainly wasn't a child of the villages of Mazandaran. That was where her cousins lived and she lived in a different context, and yet not as different as she would have wanted it to be.

As an only child and a Tehrani, Nahal was an ordinary little girl compared to all other ten-year-olds with middle-class parents in Tehran in 1977. She had short hair that hugged her chubby, round face closely. If you were in the know you would describe it as a John Lennon haircut. Nahal was too young or too ordinary or too Iranian to know about John Lennon. She didn't even own a tape recorder, leave alone any tapes. The only pop stars she had heard of were Donny and Marie Osmond and that was thanks to the older American-Iranian girls at her American Community School.

Nahal had divided the girls in her school into three types. The first type were like her, Iranian-Iranian. That meant that they came from middle-class Iranian families who held true to their Iranian culture, spent their holidays in Iran and read Persian poetry for entertainment. These girls spoke Farsi at home, ate Persian food and were not allowed to have sleepovers. Their parents maintained a Persian context, even though they sent their daughters to an American School.

The second type were the American-Iranian girls. These girls were pseudo-Americans. They had a totally different context. Their parents were or wanted to be connected to America in some shape or form. And so did their girls. These girls knew all about Hershey chocolate bars, shopped at the newly opened Super Schelan supermarket in Tehran, and watched the Osmonds and Mickey Mouse Club on the American TV channel. Their parents insisted on speaking American English at home and school holidays were filled with ski trips and Disneyland. In reality, they were better than the American-Americans but they just didn't know it or couldn't make the distinction.

Last and definitely not least were the American-American girls. These girls didn't need to pretend. They were the genuine article. The very best that New York could export. They ranked at the top of the hierarchy in Nahal's kingdom. They bullied the Iranian-Iranian girls like Nahal, often supported by their American-Iranian cronies. In the evenings they went back to empty homes with chocolate-chip cookies, Sloppy Joe burgers and Hershey bars for dinner. School was only a showcase for their context as they broke the rules, scored the lowest marks, wore the best of the worst clothes, and acted as if they didn't care. And why should they? No one else could do the American-American thing as well as they could and they knew it.

The truth was that Nahal didn't want to be one of them; she just didn't know or didn't want to know that she wasn't. It's difficult to explain this and she never really tried. Maybe if she was at school with her Mazandarani cousins, then she would have been happy being the same as everyone else. For now at least she was not a happy ten-year-old and that is the beginning of her story.

Sara spotted Nahal at the front of the school bus sitting next to the driver. Some of the ninth-grade American-American boys were shouting at her from the second and third rows. Nahal was sitting very still. Not a single muscle, not a single sound. And yet Sara could feel her anger and humiliation. Something about the child screamed defiance at those ninth-grade bullies. They were poking fun at her hair, her size, her bag, her shoes and the fact that she sat next to the driver, with screams of 'Teacher's pet, scaredy cat, go and tell your daddy that . . .'

The chanting was giving everyone a headache. Sara had had enough of the spectacle. She didn't know Nahal but she had a compelling desire to scream back at the bullies. 'God, you lot make me sick. Why don't you just shut the fuck up and pick on someone your own size?' she said slowly and loudly as the bus stopped in the school yard.

Sara was the same age as Nahal but somehow she looked older. She had a confidence and brashness about her that was so typically New York – a real American-American.

She also had four older brothers and she knew all there was to know about dealing with bullies. The ninth-graders were caught off-guard and scattered out of the bus, deflated.

Nahal was the last to leave the bus even though she was sitting right next to the exit. She seemed to defrost as she scrambled out. Sara was waiting for her in front of the bus. She was clutching her schoolbag to her chest for some sort of protection. Her face was covered with sheepdog red and brown ringlets that hid her freckles. Now that she was off the bus she didn't feel so brave, and wasn't sure if she should be seen talking to Nahal. But before she knew it, Nahal was standing next to her.

'Thank you, Sara.'

'No problem, they had it coming. I was getting a head-ache,' muttered Sara, wondering how Nahal knew her name.

The girls made their way towards the school building. 'How do you know my name?' quizzed Sara.

Nahal smiled for the first time. 'We are in the same English class. You know, Mrs Echerd's grammar, first period? We meet every day.'

Sara felt guilty. She hadn't really noticed Nahal before that day, either in the bus or in class. She was often too busy dozing or copying her homework off someone else to pay attention in class. She didn't even know her name. 'Oh yeah, I know. We better dash if we are going to make Old Echerd's roll call.'

The school's forecourt was empty. Not a child in sight. Black autumn clouds hung low over the floor of tarmac as the wind whispered strange warnings through the giant pines.

Two little figures could be seen walking silently towards the school building. You might think they were friends just from the way they walked together, keeping perfect time as if they had done the same walk for many years. Their silence might have disturbed you, but then you can never tell with girls. You might have thought they were sisters, but they looked so different. The lanky, sturdy limbs of the redhead dwarfed the chubby, dark-haired little figure. You might have a feeling that something was missing or amiss, like a technically perfect painting in which something about the composition lacked soul and life. And you would be right.

Maybe it was because Nahal was an only child. Or maybe it had something to do with Sara being the only girl of five children. Maybe it was the Iranian-Iranian opposite attracting the American-American. Whatever the reason, and however it happened, Nahal and Sara became friends.

It was a quiet friendship. Theirs wasn't the loud banter of other little girls. If you didn't look you would not see it. Nahal sat silently next to Sara on the school bus. Sara waited for Nahal after her science period and they shared lunch in a quiet corner of their form room.

Nahal always had something wrapped in Persian nan bread for lunch. She hated her lunches. It was so embarrassing not to have real sandwich bread, not to be the same as the other kids. And then her mum put too much butter on the bread so you couldn't taste the filling, invariably Persian goat cheese.

To Nahal, Sara's lunch seemed exciting and full of promise. There were peanut butter sandwiches, thinly buttered on cut, white sandwich bread, all neatly squashed into aluminium foil. Then Sara had a packet of cheesy crisps and chocolate or fruit. Sara laughed at the way Nahal hid her Iranian sandwiches and devoured her peanut butter concoction. What she failed to tell Nahal was that she made the sandwiches herself every day because her mother could never get over her hangover early enough to make her sandwiches. Anyway, Sara didn't really like peanut butter and given half a chance would have picked on the Persian goat cheese wraps – but Nahal never gave her the chance. She made it look as if it was uncool even to look at her lunch. The irony was that many years later some innovative entrepreneur would make goat cheese wraps the trendiest lunchtime dish in the best restaurants everywhere in the world, apart from Tehran.

The girls' friendship deepened in spite of these contradictions. They began to develop an imaginary world of their own. Sara was the leader. She would pretend to connect with a spirit world and, holding Nahal's hands, would make up magic spells that they would both recite in their morning recess. Dancing round and round on the same spot, they looked like little dervishes. Gazing up to the sky, they focused on the tallest pine tree. As they became dizzier and dizzier, Sara would utter and mutter her spell before falling to the ground with sheer exhaustion. Then Nahal would follow suit. In those moments of dizziness Sara claimed to contact the devil and ask him for a list of things which included a near perfect maths homework, an A for science and a day's illness for Mrs Echerd, not to mention untold mishaps for the ninth-grade bullies.

Sara's mother was a fortune-teller of Irish, gipsy blood. Madame Moon spent most of her days reading the fortunes of gullible Iranian wives. These superstitious women believed that this red-haired American could connect with their stars, and the ghosts of past lives. A favourite pastime of the Iranian-Americans was to invite Mrs Moon to their socialite evening parties, where she drank her way into impressive trances of fortune-telling mania every night. Her fortune-telling income was what kept her and Sara in the style they had become accustomed to after her husband left her in disgust a few years ago, taking his sons with him.

Sara never understood why her father didn't take her as well. She assumed it was because she was the youngest – too young to travel back to New York. The truth was much more complex. Her father was not her father. She was an accident of the kind of night that her mother never seemed to see in her crystal ball in spite of their frequency. So, if you thought about it, it really wasn't Sara's fault. Given this context she was bound to revert to supernatural powers for help.

Winter came and went, as did spring and summer. And so a year passed during which Sara and Nahal developed an unsustainable intensity to their friendship. They began to spend all their time together. They were best friends.

And then one red, cold September morning Sara did not get on the bus. Nahal was hurt. She couldn't understand it. Where was Sara? Why hadn't she told her she wasn't coming to school? Was she ill? Why hadn't she called her to let her know? She so desperately wanted to talk to Sara, she so desperately needed her American-American friend.

You see, this was no ordinary day. Nahal started the day with red, runny, blood all over her knickers. It was the day of her first period. Her mother had told her very little about periods and menstrual cycles. She hadn't expected her little girl to grow up quite so quickly. She told her even less on the day except to give her a rather large, sausage-like thing called a 'pad' to stick on to her knickers all day 'to stop the blood'. Her mother also gave her a spare pad in case her existing one became too bloody and told her not to mention this to anybody. 'It's a female curse, Nahal,' she said.

Nahal begged her mother to let her stay at home until the curse passed. Her mother laughed at her. 'It's a lifelong curse, Nahal, and the sooner you accept it the better.' Nahal didn't bother to ask any more questions after that. She threw the pad to the bottom of her school bag. She would talk to Sara about it, Sara would know what to do. Nahal was sure that Sara's mum would have told her all the details and shown her all the necessary counter-curses and spells. Maybe, just maybe, Sara could lift this lifelong curse after all.

Nahal spent the day confused and worried. She couldn't concentrate and was the first to drop out in the spelling bee. Mrs Echerd was not pleased. Alone in recess, Nahal looked around for familiar faces but didn't recognise anyone. Nahal and Sara spent so much time together, they had grown oblivious of the other girls and boys around them. Nahal went to their secret spot at the back of the school. Gazing at the tallest pine she tried to mutter one of their magic spells but without Sara nothing seemed to work. The magic was gone.

On the ride back home, she sat at the back of the bus where she usually sat with Sara. She thought about ringing Sara at home that night. Nahal's mother didn't like her to use the phone, but surely this was an exception? Her thoughts were disturbed by a somewhat familiar chant. A group of boys were standing in front of her and poking her with a ruler. 'Who is this then? Our high and mighty smelly girl? All alone are we? Where is your bosom buddy now? Gone and left you, has she? Couldn't stand your cheesy smell?'

Nahal was scared but she was determined not to show it. She wanted to get out of the bus but she was right at the back and she would have to manoeuvre her way down the narrow central aisle past the bullies. Without Sara there to protect her she felt displaced and vulnerable, as if she was in a place where she didn't belong and was certainly not wanted.

One of the American-American boys grabbed her school bag and started to throw it to the front of the bus. The boys passed the bag around the bus. The American-American girls started to join in. Nahal was feeling dizzy and disorientated. Who should she chase, what should she do, where was Sara? Bradley, the Apollo-like leader of the American-American gang, came up to Nahal. Tall and blond, his sixteen-year-old frame towered over Nahal, dwarfing her. He held the bag above her head, his long, white arms stretched skywards beyond her reach. 'You want it, smelly girl, you jump for it.'

It was an invitation to battle and humiliation. Nahal didn't know what to do. She couldn't look Bradley in the eye. His eyes were crystal blue, cold and lifeless and yet they stirred strong emotions of resistance and defiance in Nahal. It was the way he looked at her, as if he had a God-given right to torture her. Nahal wasn't sure of many things but she was sure that she would not and should not give in to Bradley.

'Just give it back, it's mine and you have no right,' she said quietly. She didn't care about the bag but she didn't want them to find the pad. She didn't want them to know that she had a curse. Bradley smiled, the cracks disrupting the perfect plaster of his thin, angular face. He opened the bag and turned it upside down. The pad fell to the floor with a thud along with her books and papers. It was a loud thud. Bradley whistled, picked up the pad slowly and held it up for everyone to see like an auctioneer with a prized antique. The bus got noisier and noisier as the audience bid against each other for the nastiest comment.

Finally, Bradley came closer. He bent down, stooping low, until he was staring into Nahal's eyes. She refused to look at him, gazing instead into the nothingness of his pale face. He dangled the pad in front of her, edging it towards her face until her nose touched the material. 'Smelly girl,' he said and then walked away laughing. 'Come and see our smelly girl, everyone.' This time she had the whole bus around her pointing and poking and laughing all at the same time. Their faces seemed to get larger and larger as Nahal shrank further and further into her seat. She felt claustrophobic, as if she was suffocating. She needed air. Bradley made red pen marks all over her pad and put it on her lap. 'Don't you need a new pad, smelly girl?'

The traffic lights turned red as they approached the top of her road. Nahal was on the final run. Only a few more minutes and she would be in the safety of her house. The bus driver had been driving too fast; he almost missed the red light and had to jam on the brakes. The bus came to a sudden halt. And then it happened. Something snapped in Nahal. She got up as if shocked into action, and screamed in a mixture of English and Persian, 'My name is Nahal, you bloody American bastard.' It was a scream of repressed anger, long and hot and loud. But it seemed to freeze and then vanish into the silence of the bus as if someone had pressed the pause button at the scariest point in a film. All eyes were fixed on a point and that point seemed to be somewhere on Nahal. She followed their gaze in slow motion, taking in every face, every eye, every centimetre of suspense. And then she knew. She didn't need to see what they saw. She could feel it, trickling down the inside of her legs. She was covered in blood.

The bus came to a gentle stop just outside Nahal's home. The door opened. Nahal looked up in an effort to focus. She saw Sara standing at the foot of the steps to the bus, waiting to come and meet her friend. Nahal could tell that Sara was excited about something but she couldn't muster the energy to greet her friend. She stood there, a volcanic eruption frozen with shock, unable to move.

The silence that greeted Sara drew her attention to the back of the bus. There she saw her friend standing, glued to the spot, motionless. Sara looked at the other children on the bus, demanding an explanation. No one dared hold her gaze. The bus driver came up behind Sara and muttered something in Persian. *'Tagserh Bradley, pesar badgensh be namosh.'* Sara didn't understand Farsi but she understood enough to look at Bradley.

'Don't look at me,' he mumbled. 'Your friend is a total nutcase. I was just having a bit of fun.'

Sara didn't seem to need any further explanation. She gestured with her middle finger to Bradley, 'You asshole.' Sara then walked over to Nahal and wrapped her coat around her and led her gently off the bus towards the freedom of Nahal's own home.

This was the first time that Sara had been to Nahal's home. It was a moment of mixed emotions for both girls. Sara was curious about the scenes and secrets that Nahal was hiding. Nahal was uncertain about introducing Sara to the centre of her Iranian-Iranian world, as embarrassed about the Persian essence of her home as she was of her Iranian-Iranian goat cheese wrap.

They walked down a narrow, dusty alleyway that ended in an intricate, iron gate of entangled sixteenth-century Persian designs. Protected on either side by high brick walls, they could taste, smell and sense the sweet lime and tangy lemon trees that lay behind this ornate Persian gateway to paradise.

The girls stood with their backs to the gate holding hands, refusing to face their mutual fears for a little longer. The sun was setting on the hills of Tehran, gently caressing the peaks. The warm glow of the evening sunset gave Nahal a little courage. She was the first to speak.

'Where were you, Sara? I needed you.'

'My father came back with my brothers, Nahal. Mum and Dad are going to try again. We are going to be a family. I spent the day helping my brothers unpack.' Sara tried to sound flat but she couldn't suppress a hint of excitement in her voice. 'I am sorry,' she added. 'I am really, really sorry, Nahal.'

Nahal didn't reply straightaway. Finally, she realised that it was getting dark and her mother would be worrying. 'I am glad I am an Iranian, Sara,' Nahal said testingly. Sara smiled, 'You know what, that is just what I was thinking, Nahal.' Sara turned and faced the gate, pulling Nahal around at the same time.

'Come on, ring the bell to this palace, I could kill one of your mum's goat cheese sandwiches.'

Nahal couldn't resist a smile. 'Mum is too afraid to buy anything but peanut butter now.'

Sara looked at her in disbelief. 'You cannot be serious!' They both started to laugh, hungry for their Iranian-American peanut butter goat cheese wrap.

maddox

MONICA TAYLOR

'MORNING!' yelled the night officer through the hatch.

No answer from the cell.

'Halloo! Can you move your leg or hand or anything, please,' the night officer yelled again.

No answer, no movement from the cell.

'Halloooo! Hey!! Can you hear me? Could you please move your hand, head or leg please,' the officer repeated. All she wanted was to make sure the girl inside was still alive before she went off-duty.

'Hey!!! Shut up, you don't have to yell at me like that. I heard you, can't someone enjoy her sleep here? It's only 6.30 a.m. Shit,' came a voice from the cell.

It seemed that Maddox hated being woken up in the morning. She had trouble getting to sleep at night and she always caught up on her sleep in the morning.

It had taken the officer five minutes just to get Maddox to yell at her. Duty done, she went on to the next cell. 'At least she's still alive,' the officer said to herself as she opened the next cell's hatch, and yelled, 'Morning!'

Maddox was about to fall asleep after the night officer had passed when there was another set of keys in the hatch lock. The day officer was opening to yell her 'Morning!' It was always at 7.15 that they did this.

This seemed to be more than the inmate could take. 'Now, you bloody screw!' yelled Maddox. 'Open that hatch and yell your "morning" to me, if you want to see my hand smashing your nose!'

Maddox was a common element in this place. Most of the officers knew full well that they shouldn't open the hatch. Only new officers fell for it. But those who had seen Maddox on her previous stops in the place knew better. In fact she spent most of her stays in the prison down in the punishment block. Whatever you did or said, Maddox didn't give a shit about the consequences. Block or no block, the shit hole was a shit hole.

She went back to sleep, murmuring, 'Bloody screws, motherfuckers, never let you sleep. Fuck them.'

When you met Maddox in the corridors of the prison, you'd step aside to let her pass, fearing that you might be the next person she'd smash on the nose. Unless you knew her, you'd never come near her. Mad? Yes, she was, but when you came to know her, she was a normal person and as caring as you yourself.

She made sure, though, that most of the time people left her alone. She also had a way of fucking the law, or rather the judges were tired of seeing her in their courts. In the twenty times she had been in custody and in the courts, only seven times did she get a conviction and a sentence. And each time she went down with a different name: Dana, Caroline, Steph, Justice, Amber, Nicky, to name a few . . .

Well, you can call them sentences, but most of them were between one month and a maximum of four months. But each time she was in custody, the governors had to add days on to her sentences or her days in custody as she always made sure she'd get them to put her down the block.

The law of the prison was that if you committed an offence in prison you had days added on to your sentence. This was no problem to Maddox and they knew it. Sometimes she even did it intentionally, just because towards the end of her sentence she fell in love with another girl and didn't want to leave her.

In this women's prison, association was almost every day at 5.30 p.m. till 7.45 p.m. And this day was one of them, so Jenny ran to the bathroom as she knew the queue would be long if she didn't rush.

On association you could bathe, make a phone call, or watch the TV which was in the association room – though it was difficult to watch as you had to agree with sixty other women who wanted to watch it as well.

But, as always, every two days when they had association, Jenny ran to the bathroom to have her shower. And, as always, she was honest to those around her and those she cared for. When she entered the bathroom, she found a watch, a necklace and a bracelet that one of the girls had forgotten. When Jenny went to bathe, she left her things inside to keep her turn at the bathroom – this was the trick if you wanted to bathe, though some weird ones could come and remove your things and take your turn. So Jenny prayed no one would turn up. In fact, most women had given up the idea of bathing in the bathroom and decided to bathe from the washbasins in their cells.

Jenny left the bathroom and went to the screws' office which was next door to the bathroom, opposite the association room.

'Excuse me, sir,' Jenny called to one of the officers who was sitting in the office.

'Hang on,' he said without turning to look at her.

Jenny waited for two minutes as Mr Smith chatted with the other officer.

'Sir,' Jenny tried again.

'In a minute,' Mr Smith said. He really seemed to have something against Jenny, yet all the other officers liked her and helped her the best they could. But Mr Smith really hated her.

'Yes, Jenny,' the other officer said. 'What can we do for you?' Mr Smith looked at her as if she was rubbish.

'Excuse me, sir. I found these items in the bathroom, someone must have forgotten them there. Could you find the owner and hand them to her?'

'All right, Jenny, give them to me.'

Jenny handed him the items and left the office. Mr Smith didn't say 'thank you' or look her way.

She went back to the bathroom, bathed and went back to her dormitory cell which she shared with three other girls. She liked them all. Sheryl and Nadine talked only about pipes, rocks, grass, chocolate and all these terms which Jenny had never come across in her life before. Sarah also knew what they were talking about, but for Jenny, a pipe was just a pipe. So one night she asked Sheryl what a pipe was. And to everyone's surprise, Jenny really knew nothing about drugs. Sheryl tried to explain but Jenny couldn't get what a pipe was. In the end Sheryl decided to draw the pipe for her.

All these girls were wealthy at one time in their lives but went down with drugs testing. Sarah was just starting while Sheryl and Nadine had been inside fifteen times. To Jenny they were good girls who took wrong turns in their lives. And they treated Jenny with respect as she was the eldest in the dorm. Though in all they were lazy when it came to cleaning the dorm. But they always made sure that every-thing was fine with the whole group.

When she was ready, Jenny went to make a call to her children and waited in the queue as everyone did. Everyone had five minutes on the phones, so you really didn't have much to say apart from 'Hello,' and 'I love you,' or 'I hate you.' After her call she went back to her dorm. She liked staying in her dorm as it limited the chances of her getting into trouble.

Jenny sat down at the only table for everyone and wrote a letter to her pen-friend who was in another prison. She was busy writing when the shout came: 'Hot water! Last call for the hot water!' If you were late the kitchen was locked, meaning no hot water for you. Then it was time for bang-up. This was from 7.45 p.m. to 8 a.m. – that was if the officers were on time. Though on the weekends it was always 8.30 when they opened the cells. Poor officers, they had to do it door by door, not forgetting they have sixty women on one wing to watch.

'Goodnight!' shouted the night officer. They had been banged in for over an hour and a half.

'Goodnight!' shouted Jenny and the girls in the dorm, and the officer continued on to his next cell.

'Morning,' shouted the same officer before he went off duty at 6.30 a.m. At 8 a.m. the officer opened the doors. 'Morn-ing! Time for breakfast!'

Jenny and the other girls went for breakfast. While Jenny was eating, someone came to stand at her table.

'Hello,' the other girl said.

'Hello!' Jenny said, then lifted her head to look at the

person standing there, and was surprised to see that it was Maddox.

Maddox was five foot ten, with Rasta hair on the left side of her head and bald on the right side. Due to an operation, her hair wouldn't grow on that side. Her eyes, when directed at you, were menacing and huge in their sockets; you wouldn't look twice at her.

'Can I help you?' Jenny asked, not knowing what to say to the mad girl of the wing.

'No,' Maddox said and sat in front of Jenny.

Jenny, puzzled, just looked at her and never showed the worry that was building up inside her. She was by then not hungry any more, and was asking herself the questions she should have asked Maddox, like, 'What did I do?' Or 'What does she want?' or, 'Oh God, let her not say she loves me!' As this was one of Maddox's hobbies, collecting girls. But Jenny knew though that she preferred young girls, not women like Jenny herself.

'I just wanted to say thank you. I came to your dorm last night but you were not in – I think you had gone for your bloody stupid hot water. Anyway, thank you,' Maddox said.

'Thanks for what?' Jenny asked.

'For my watch and all the other things you gave to the officer,' Maddox replied.

'It's nothing.' Jenny didn't show it, but she was relieved.

'No, love, if it was another girl she would have kept all the things and traded them for something else. Really, thanks, you're too honest to be in this shit hole with these bloody screws. Fuck them, always looking for trouble where I'm concerned. Thanks, love, and I'll be there if you need me.' Maddox stood up and left Jenny staring at her. It wasn't like Maddox to say 'thank you'. This was new to Jenny. It took some minutes for it to sink in.

'Time to clean your rooms!' shouted the officer. It was now 8.15 a.m. Imagine just fifteen minutes for breakfast and to clean up before exercise, which took place from 8.30 a.m. to 9 a.m.

Jenny went to the dorm and helped all the others to clean it.

'Exercise!' came the officers' call. 'Everyone for exercise in the dining room.'

'Oh no, we haven't finished and he's calling,' Jenny said.

'Go if you want, I'll finish up,' said Sarah.

'You're sure?' asked Jenny.

'Sure! You'd better go before that bad boy calls again.'

'Okay! Thanks, Sarah. I'll do the general cleaning on Saturday.' On Saturday, you had to clean behind all the cupboards, move everything in the room, as they inspected everything, even the floor behind the cupboards. And Jenny always did this cleaning with the girls, though she was the one who did most of it.

'No problem, you always do it anyway. Go! Go! They're going to lock you in if you don't go,' Sarah urged her.

'How many?' asked the S.O. to the officer on duty through the walkie-talkie. The girls were gathered in the dining room ready to go.

'Twelve, Miss Grant,' he answered.

'All right, bring them down.'

'Exercise' was a garden where you go to breathe some air. All you could do in this garden was to sit and talk to the other inmates or walk around the garden until they called you back inside at 9 a.m. The exercise yard was between four walls, two of which were the wings, with the barred cell windows and the others backed on to the prison car park and the back of the canteen. The space was only about nine metres square, but without a choice, you had to make do with it.

Oh! Today I will just sit here, I don't want to walk and really I don't feel like talking, thought Jenny. There are days like this, when you don't feel like talking.

'A3!' called the officer, and then called again as only ten out of the twelve turned up to her first call. Maddox was standing with her new girlfriend, talking to another girl through the window which was forbidden.

Boy! Maddox changed girlfriends every day and that morning she had a new one who had just come in the night before. This was one of her hobbies! Collect as many girl-friends as she could, and girls went for her, hoping to get protection from her. Which was the error they always made. She was the one they were supposed to be protected from, though they always found out too late when she moved on to the corner.

'A!!! 3!!!' called the S.O. again. She was beginning to be upset and Maddox knew it but never moved.

'Maddox!' said Jenny, 'You'd better go in if you want to see that new jewellery of yours tomorrow.'

'A3!' called the S.O. for the last time. This time Maddox listened and went to the entrance from the garden.

'Free flow!' called the officer. 'Everyone for free-flow, in the dining room!'

The doors were opened on the education unit at 10 o'clock. They all walked to the education area, where Jenny went in for her library session.

The morning free-flow went, the afternoon one came, and they were all locked in by 4.30 p.m., until the S.O. decided whether they had association or not. That day they didn't have association due to a shortage of staff so it was bang-up for everybody.

Between 5 p.m. and 9 p.m. all prisoners had their food, hot water and all they needed for the night. At 9.30 p.m. Jenny heard shouts and banging. She didn't pay attention as this was the usual sound in prison, shouts, cries, banging, etc. Nobody really paid attention, unless it was someone you knew who was calling you through the window or hatch. Yet all this was forbidden, and if you were caught it meant hours on the block or being warned.

The shouts went on till 11 p.m. It was beyond a joke. The girl must have smashed up the whole cell, banging the remains of her chair on her door until the hatch gave way and opened itself.

Jenny heard voices in the corridor, so she got up and went to peep in the see-through line on the door. Three officers were standing in front of Maddox's cell.

Now what has upset Maddox? thought Jenny as she walked back to her bed. The banging and the screaming went on and more loud noises came from the other cell. But this was something you came to get used to and closed out of your mind. This way you stayed sane. Jenny finally managed to get some sleep.

At 7.30 in the morning, they took Maddox down the block.

When the cell doors were opened at 8 a.m. everyone who was going to the servery for breakfast stopped to peep into Maddox's room. This was a scene you would have dreaded to see in your own home. The mattress was gone, the pillow gone, and all the covers. They found out later they had been pushed through the window and were lying three levels down on the ground below. The cell was all flooded and the water came out into the corridor where the women passed when they were out of their cells. The sink and toilet were in pieces on the floor of the cell, and some bits had been hurled out of the window. Had Maddox been stronger, the pipes would have come out as she had tried to pull at them. If ever you needed a house demolition, just contact Maddox, thought Jenny.

Jenny was ready for free-flow as all the cell doors opened and one of the officers who always teased her came in.

'Jenny!' Mrs Harper called.

'Yes, miss!' this was the easiest thing to call them, because putting names on all of them was too much of a hassle.

'Do you mind going down the block and having a word with your friend? She's still upset. That's if you don't mind.'

Jenny knew that when you worked as a listener you could never turn down a call, unless what you were doing was more important. Though you had a right to say no if you were not on duty. But as Jenny knew who was calling, she thought it better to go and see her.

'No! I don't mind, miss. Just give me a few moments to put on my uniform.'

'Thanks Jenny. I'll tell them when you are coming.' She left the cell then, leaving it open for Jenny to come out when ready.

Listeners had a red jersey or T-shirt with a logo on it. They also carried a badge with their photograph and name. Jenny was in the office in less than five minutes.

'Ready, miss,' she said, and the officer came to open the landing door so that Jenny could go downstairs to where the block wing was located.

The stairs that led to the block were not very well lit. They were dark, cold, and seemed to be out of use, which made them scary for anyone going down there for the first time.

On arrival she banged on the landing door so that they could let her in. The officer came and opened the door for her. He led the way to Maddox's new cell. Here, most of the hatches were opened by officers but you could find some which you could open with the end of a plastic spoon. In fact, Jenny had broken one spoon and carried the end around with her when she was on duty. But today the officer opened it for her.

'Maddox, you've got a visitor,' he called through the hatch.

'I don't want to see any bloody visitor or listener, I told you already,' Maddox shouted back.

'Well, she's here. Let me know when you're through,' the officer said to Jenny, then went back to the office.

'Hello Maddox!' said Jenny through the hatch, seeing her lying on the bed with covers pulled up to her head.

'I said I don't want to see anyone,' Maddox said without looking at the door. It looked like she had decided to lie on her bed all day as she hadn't had any sleep the whole night.

'Maddox!' called Jenny. 'It's me, Jenny.'

Maddox lifted the covers from her head to check on the caller before saying anything harsh.

'Well, you don't want to see me either?' Jenny asked her.

'Ah! It's you! I just don't want to talk,' Maddox replied.

Jenny didn't take it personally, as she came across this statement often while on duty as a listener. Most girls never wanted to talk.

'OK, I'll just stay here for a few minutes, then I'll leave you alone. Is that OK with you?' Jenny asked.

'All right.' Maddox got out of bed and came to the hatch, where Jenny could see her face, but not the lower part of her body. 'Sorry, Jenny, they just piss me off, these stupid officers.'

'You don't have to be sorry. You know I understand when people don't want to talk. It happens to me, you know.'

'Thanks for coming, anyway.'

'Tell me, what happened?'

'That bitch, that bitch, she nicked me!' Maddox explained. 'That slut, I'll kill her! She grassed. She went and told the screw that I had some chocolate and some grass. And I was at the window enjoying the puff when the bitch peeped in the hatch and got the smell right in her face. Bloody bastard, she nicked me.'

'So you decided to smash your presidential suite?'

'No, after she nicked me, they came in the cell for a room search. That girl taped up everything.'

'Uh huh.'

'Yes darling, the usual stuff.'

'M'mm. Was it much they nicked?'

'Ha, ha, ha! Jenny! You know me, don't you?'

'I guess so.' What this meant was, if you needed to sniff, Maddox was the right spot to knock at. She didn't have much of a variety, but she could get you at least three types. Grass, chocolate and a mixture of Prozac, Valium, Zimat, etc. These were costly in the walls of this prison. No money changed hands, but items like phone cards, stamps, tobacco and other things. Maddox had all the things you could trade. Which meant they not only found drugs but other things that had other girls' prison numbers. When these were found in your possession, they also got you nicked.

'So! Have you seen the governor yet?'

'No! Not yet. But I'm used to the situation. They're going to add more days on my sentence.'

True to her word, Maddox was always down the block, for one reason or another. Fighting with the officers, possession of drugs, shouting through the window, and oh! her speciality – collecting girls. Each day she had a new girl she was kissing and she was always nicked while making love with one of them. Though, this time, it was for drugs.

'How many days do you think you might get?'

'Maybe three, or one week. But I don't give a damn. Know what, Jenny, I will walk from court, so they can put those days where I think. Fuck them, Jenny.'

'I had forgotten you're in court soon.'

'Yes, love, and I'm walking. Trust me.'

'Well, I hope you do. Anyway, it's thirty minutes since I've been here. I have to go now. You know the regulations, I can't spend more than fifteen minutes with one inmate.'

'Yeah! Idiot regulations.'

'I'll go now.' But as she was about to go, Maddox turned to one side and Jenny noticed a line on her neck which was more visible on the right side. Jenny asked what she had done to get the mark on her neck. Without answering her, Maddox showed Jenny her arm and wrists. Jenny couldn't stop herself from asking the question that had popped into her mind after noticing the mark on her neck. 'By the way, you aren't thinking of killing yourself, are you?'

'Hey! Darling, you know I'll never kill myself. Self harm, yes, but not kill myself.'

Jenny didn't ask if she had tried to do it last night or earlier that day. Instead, she asked if she would harm herself again.

'It helps me release the pain, Jenny. From time to time

I feel like doing it, but now that I've talked to you, I feel better.'

'You know that you can call any of us listeners if you need to talk to somebody. OK? Don't hesitate if you want to talk.'

'I'll call, I promise.'

'All right, then, I'll go now. See you later, heh?' Jenny reported to the officer that she was leaving and the officer let her off the wing.

Two days later, Maddox was returned to the wings, but not to the same wing as before. So all Jenny could hear of her as she didn't see her on free-flow – because she always managed to make them ban her from going anywhere – was the shouts through the windows to her girlfriends, 'I fucking love you, see you on exercise, I miss you.'

So that was the Maddox Jenny came to know briefly, just by handing back her things.

As a listener, Jenny had two or three chances to see her after she came up from the block. And a week later, Maddox went to court and, as she had said to Jenny that day down the block, after a few hours in court the judge said, 'Case dismissed.'

The funniest thing in all this was that she had told Jenny the truth. She was guilty! And there she walked, again!

With a smile Jenny mused to herself, 'Let's see how long she'll stay away from this place.'

getting away from mama

PAMELA VINCENT

AUGUST AND THE PAVEMENT on Pitkin Avenue, Brooklyn, is steaming. You can smell the asphalt cooking. All through the day you can hear the shouting and laughter of kids outside: they've jammed the fire hydrant to make a cool shower to run through. We have the windows open in our basement room. Mama has to clean the whole big house in return for our single room. We share the bathroom and kitchen with everyone else. She's upstairs in the bathroom, right now, finishing off some of the laundry she takes in.

I have just lain down on our bed, exhausted from working as a waitress in The Sandwich Shoppe in Manhattan. At least my job takes me away from Mama's world, from Brooklyn. But at just fifteen, what do I know of sandwiches, smandwiches? You ask for tuna on rye, I give you tuna on white, what's the big deal? And the sandwiches have names – can you believe it? 'The Belvedere', 'The Swiss Chalet', I ask you! I'm always getting them mixed up. I'm pretty enough, you know, with grey-blue eyes and olive skin. I can get away with almost anything with most of the men. With the women, it's a different story. Some hate me, cordially, on sight. At least I have the accent right. I've practised enough to wipe Brooklyn completely off my tongue.

Spread out on the bed now, enjoying the cooling air, I watch the sky turning from orange to black behind the tenements framed by the window. I'm thinking about a woman in a purple hat in the restaurant today. Her face turns the same colour as her hat when the man she' s with winks at me. I've brought the wrong kind of coffee – what do I know about coffee? There's white coffee and there's black, right?

At the bedroom window there's a shadow, which gets larger, more distinct. It's the shape of a large, bare-chested man, maybe six feet tall, black against the night sky – I can see every muscle. What's he doing, climbing in through the window now? Too scared to scream, I just lie still on the bed, curling into myself, my body beginning to feel hard and strange, like someone else's used chewing gum. Then, at the doorway, another shape – small, barely five feet tall, roundly female. It's my mother, Sadie, with a foot-long carving knife in her hands, the tip pointing at that unknown man. A butcher's daughter, she knows how to handle a knife!

Nothing is said. She just stands there. The man-shape climbs out of the window, but not before she's just scratched the skin of his chest with the tip of her blade. He's clutching himself. Then she puts down the knife, closes the window, and goes over to me. '*Fagela*,' she says, using that Yiddish diminutive, 'little bird', that I hate, 'are you all right?' Why can't she call me 'Frances', or at least 'Fanny' like everyone else? I am going to go to Hunter College next year, after all.

Still, I owe her. She's saved the life she gave me in the first place. *Chutzpah* – it's a Yiddish word – do you know what it means? I guess you'd call it 'nerve' or even 'cheek' – but all of that's too weak to describe it. Well my Mama has it, in spades.

With her snub nose, blue button eyes and pink rubber cheeks, she looks like a baby doll. I have my father's black hair, strong chin and straight nose – nothing like hers. She looks more like my sister than my mother, despite her hair. It turned white when she was thirty-five and now, in the moonlight, it looks like new-laid snow.

We never got along. When I was two years old, my mother gave me a yellow sweater with a lace trim. I hate fancy things, so, all by myself, I found my way to a playground far away and buried it in the sandpit. At about the same time, she paid for a photo of me on a horse, but I refused to smile. My mother always smiles. Get the picture? What turned her hair white? It was the deaths of my father, a policeman, when I was four, and then of my little brother, when I was eleven. So I am all that my mother has. She turns the full beam of her powerful love on me, like a searchlight, holds on to me the way a fierce little dog clenches a bone in its teeth.

Anyway, a few years after my mother frightens away the rapist, I meet Nate and escape from my mother seems possible. I'm sitting on the stoop in Pitkin Avenue with my friend Shirley. It's another simmering night. This tall young man with glasses and thick, dark curls walks past, waves, then turns around and comes back. He takes another look at me and I can see he's hooked. Shirley has already told me how great he is – the kind of good man that is so hard to find. He asks me to go for a walk by the cinema on Saturday night. We don't have enough money to go to the pictures but at least we can enjoy looking at the stills together. Over the next few weeks he asks me, not once, but three times, to marry him. When I find out how many other girls are after him, I think I'd better not hang around! Nate is a scientist, being hauled off to work on some project for the government in Washington, D.C. Better grab him before someone else does!

Shirley is crying at our wedding reception in a little room above a candy store on Pitkin Avenue – and it isn't from happiness. September 1st, 1939, but it's as hot as August, so I'm leaning out of the open window. I see a whole crowd of people on the pavement who seem to be looking up at me. Now, I know I look gorgeous in my rented wedding-gown, but not that gorgeous! I stick my head out further for my admiring throng – and see they're looking up, above the window. There's a big sign saying that war has been declared. I have no idea how it will change all our lives. A conflict closer to home preoccupies me now.

A week later, freedom! I am away from my mother for the first time in my life. Nate and I are on the shore of Lake George in upstate New York. The leaves are just beginning to turn. The sky is impossibly blue. We're camping out on the islands with other young 'lefties', one last chance to get away from it all. I'm crouching down in cold clear water, rubbing the dishes in sand. The sun is hot on my face. Nate is looking down at me adoringly, as always. I'm wearing shorts and a halter top – daring for me, then. Nate is bare-chested and without his glasses I think he looks like Johnny Weismuller.

Then, in the corner of the frame, I see something shining in the noonday sun. It's a big cooking-pot, carried by a small, round woman on the prow of a boat approaching our island. She's carrying the pot in one hand, waving at us with the other. You guessed it – Sadie, cooking pot in hand. 'How did she find us?' Nate asks. I shrug my shoulders. She, who's never been out of Brooklyn since she arrived from Russia twenty-five years ago and can barely read. How did she do it?

'Mama,' I say to her, 'the people here are all young, like Nate and me.' 'So what,' is her reply. A butcher's daughter, Sadie's motto is 'meat is strength' – and meat means kosher. When I refused to eat it she threatened to pull her nails down her cheeks, saying 'Eat – or I'll tear my flesh.' 'There's no kosher meat,' I tell her now. 'So,' she says, 'I'll eat vegetables.' 'Well,' I say, 'there aren't many of them here.' 'So,' she says, 'I'll find in the woods. You'll see.' 'Mama, there's no hot water, we wash in the lake,' I say. At home everything, everybody, has to be washed in hot soapy water. I have to take baths that turn me into a boiled pullet. 'This is good clean water, like God intended,' she says. So, now she knows what God intended! 'Some of the couples here aren't married, even though they live together, have children,' I tell her. 'So?' the great Brooklyn moralist says, thumbing her nose. 'We swim naked in the lake, men and women together.' 'So,' my prudish mother says, 'you think we had bathing suits in Europe?'

I've lost. 'We have no bed or tent for you.' 'I'll make my own.' And she does. While we are registering her at the campsite, she walks out into the lake with her cooking pot and a little bread that she brought with her. She crumbles up the bread and – hey, presto – she catches a big fish in her pot. Poor Nate! He wants so much to be a big man, my Tarzan. But he catches nothing with his new, expensive rods. When it rains that night, the tent Nate has put up falls down and our bed comes apart. We are lying in the mud. The next morning we find Sadie dry and comfortable in her home-made shelter.

Nate and I load our broken bed on to a kayak he's put together, to take it to town to be fixed. 'I know I did it right,' he tells me. When we are in the middle of the lake the boat starts to let in water. 'I can't swim,' Nate says softly. 'Why didn't you tell me?' I say, 'I can't save you.' I begin to scream. Then, there is my mother, in the water, like a dolphin, pulling the boat to the shore before it sinks.

We are awakened at dawn by a launch, bringing what appears to be a dead body, covered by a discreet blanket. Seeing my mother's face, I have to admit that for a moment I feel relieved. I think (God forgive me!), 'Now, I can live my own life.' But, when I touch her cheek, her smile opens up. She'd fallen asleep on the lake and floated to the other side. '*Fagela*, it was so peaceful.'

First, she stays on our island, but our neighbour, whom Sadie calls 'the blonde', objects to her being there: 'I get the feeling Sadie's watching me, listening to me, all the time' – and she is. Sadie tells us: 'I've never seen anything like it – a woman who walks around in the nude all day and smooches with her man in the woods. That woman has a secret, you mark my words.' Sadie spits twice to avoid the evil eye. Her mother was a white witch, after all.

So, Sadie decides to join 'the bachelors', a group of men from Greenwich Village who have set up camp on an island of their own. To us they are sophisticates – the hippies of our day. Sadie befriends the sweetest of them, Saul. It is she who tells Saul's wife, a woman she calls 'Ginger Rogers' because of her red hair, how to find him.

The night before Sadie is due to go back to Brooklyn, we have a big communal bonfire. Sadie provides for it: mushrooms she picked in the woods, fish from the lake and a pile of beautiful red and green leaves which she dumps straight on the fire before anybody can stop her. After she leaves, we are all itching with the red rash of poison ivy, the toxins spread by the smoke.

Sadie accepts a cigarette from Saul. 'But, Mama,' I say, 'I didn't know you smoked.' 'There are a lot of things about me you don't know,' she says. 'I used to smoke with my brothers behind the cow-shed in the old country.' Sadie downs a couple of glasses of blackberry wine: 'This is good, like the stuff we had back home.' She gets up to dance on the table. Then I remember how she used to dance before she was married, once spending a week's wages on a feather to wear in her hair on a Saturday night. I watch her, a young, attractive, vigorous woman who has devoted her life to her daughter.

The next morning about a dozen of us are lined up at the shoreline, including 'the blonde', 'Ginger Rogers' and 'the bachelors'. We all feel the same mixture of relief and sadness. Back home, in Manhattan, 'the blonde' will introduce her new husband to the son he never knew she had. Sadie smelled out her secret, the way she could find fish in the lake and tell which of seemingly identical mushrooms was safe, which lethal.

I know that when we get back home Sadie will be waiting for us. She'll have bought chickens and made chicken soup. Later, when I paint our new apartment green, she'll repaint it dusky pink, her favourite colour, saying, 'It looked so cold.' She'll rearrange our furniture and fill our apartment with *chachkas*, the bric-a-brac she loves and I hate. When the children arrive, to her and Nate's delight and my disappointment, she'll take them over, completely. When we go camping with our kids, she'll come along. When she detects that our camping stove is about to blow up, she'll pick it up and carry it against her chest, throwing it far away from us, where it explodes. Saving all of our lives, this time. She'll teach our children to swim by throwing them into the ocean where the water is shallow, just as she taught me.

And when our kids have grown up and left, Nate and I

will try to start our own life, without her. We'll send her back to live on her own, in Brooklyn. Then she'll put her head in the gas oven – but I'll catch her just in time. She'll spend much of the rest of her life in the State Mental Home. She'll have electric shock treatment that turns her into a real baby doll – round, silent, her face smooth and expressionless.

But all of that is very far away, today. Now she is standing on the prow of a boat, waving to us all with her free hand. Her cooking pot is in the other, shining like Boadicia's shield.

paradise wharf

JOY WILKINSON

I TAKE THE LIFT to the fifteenth floor, look both ways along the corridor to make sure no one is watching, then I begin. With my toes right up to the locked front door, I let my body drop back till it hits the opposite wall. The wall is bare stone with no blown vinyl or flock wallpaper to soften the blow so when my spine hits it I wince with pain, but I don't make a sound. I never do. Slowly, pushing my smarting back bump by bony bump into the stone, I walk my blinding white trainers up the front door until I'm a tightrope, parallel to the floor. I can feel the tension in my bent knees just waiting to be freed so, holding my breath, I straighten them. The door gasps and pops open like the escape hatch on a rocket, sucked out into space. In seconds, the door is shut again and I'm inside the flat. I've entered hundreds of flats this way, but this one is different, I can tell straightaway from the smell.

The hallway smells of damp and ashtrays and rancid pans, but I am used to those smells and quite like them. I reckon smell is my strongest sense and that's fine by me. I'd take the blinding high of spray-paint or the liquorice sting of an early morning cigarette over a nice view or tune any day. There are hardly any smells I don't like, except for dog shit and school which are pretty much interchangeable, but this smell, even though it's only faint, this smell I definitely don't like.

Taking shallow breaths, I creep along the hallway. I'd pressed the buzzer three times, but this is still no guarantee that no one is home. People in these flats don't always answer their doors and I don't blame them. There are worse people than me on the prowl around Bermondsey. There are worse people than me living in these flats. When I started out, I broke into a dealer's flat and came out with a broken rib and bust lip to prove it. Now the dealers are easier to spot with their barricaded doors and Fort Knox letter boxes, but you can't spot the drunks, the killers, the perverts, who might be listening to the buzzer and grinning in wait. Now I'm thinking of them and remembering the Channel Five shows about boys buried under floorboards or rotting in bathtubs with holes drilled in their skulls and their gizzards in the oven. Is that what the smell is? Cooking guts? It could be. I've never smelt it before but my guts are curling up.

I pass the door into the kitchen and nudge it open wide enough to see that no pans of flesh are bubbling on the hob. A few pots are crusted up on the sink but the room is still and empty and cold enough to have been empty a long time. The smell is less strong here, but I can't stay in the kitchen. My dad doesn't want cutlery and kettles. The booty is in living rooms and bedrooms and, near Christmas, in cubbyholes, attics and airing cupboards. As I leave the kitchen and go towards the living room door, the stink thickens.

The moonlight is trapped behind dirty net curtains. The room is as cold as bone. There's hardly any furniture: a bedsettee slumps half-unfolded and an electric fire sprouts wires where the plug should be. There's no TV or video and I'm beginning to wonder if someone got here before me. But

I know that I'm the first person to step in this room for days, even weeks maybe. The stink says so. No one has filtered it through living lungs. A housefly darts behind the curtain and thumps against the glass. I wonder if flies have lungs.

This one must have and so must the other one that I now see orbiting the doorknob on the far side of the room. It likes what it smells and it wants to get to the source.

At the foot of the door is a small, blue shoe. Very small, not much bigger than a bootee. A baby's shoe. I think of Tink, my poor little sister, and the sickness becomes a fist in my chest.

A fly lands on my face but I don't bat it off. I'm staring at the shoe. It's smaller than the palm of my hand. I slip it in my pocket, swallow hard and slap my face harder. The fly escapes, but my cheek burns nicely, helping me to think straight.

I know now that there won't be anything my dad wants in the bedroom. I can tell that from the rips in the wallpaper in here, the map of stains on the carpet and the starving waste bins: whoever lives here has nothing. Although on the outside, these flats look like they are for the poorest of the poor, plenty of them are treasure troves. In a single day I can take home TVs, DVDs, PCs, hi-fis, mobile phones and pocketfuls of gold jewellery. The poorest of the poor really know how to spend when they do have money and even when they don't, there's always credit cards, the never-never or thieving like me. But now and again, I come across someone who has nothing, no credit or never-never, no energy for thieving or knack not to get caught. They don't want to risk a night in prison without a hit. This flat has junkie written all over it and the bedroom, where the smell is spilling like smoke, spells nothing but danger for me, I know it. But I know I'll go there anyway.

I turn the handle. The flies bump at the wood then rush through the gap as it opens. They mustn't be able to smell after all. I put my hand over my nose and go in.

The smell seeps though my fingers. I can taste it. I can almost see it. It's coming from the bed, the only thing visible in the dark. There are no net curtains in here, the window is boarded up. The bed glows like a ghost ship, the flies forming a living mist around it. Around her.

I'm close enough to see that it is a she. The sheet twisted over her forms two small peaks on her chest and swells over her belly. I daren't look at her face. The only dead face that I have ever seen was my mother's as she slept in her make-up and best dress. I don't want to think about that now.

I shut my eyes to block out the sight, but somehow this strengthens the smell, making mirages behind my eyelids. Flies of light spin in my head and the cold rushes up from the bare floor through my legs. I think I'm going to faint and see myself tumbling helplessly forward on to the bed, sinking into her chest with a soft, sickening crunch. I can't let that happen, I have to get out. I'd rather go home empty-handed and get a dead arm from Dad than let that happen.

I turn and scrabble for the door handle. My nails scrape across the paint. I claw and claw but I can't find the handle. I can't get out and all the air is dead and I can't breathe. I feel a fly brush my cheek, but I hear no sound. Was it a fly or a finger? Or a kiss?

I find the handle and turn it. Then I hear something.

A cry, but not crying. A baby's cry. Behind me.

I open the bedroom door to go, but the thought is already lead heavy in my head. I can taste the air in the living room which suddenly seems as sweet as cigarettes and chocolate. I can see the light through my eyelids, picking out bright pinks in the dark. I should run and not stop until this place is out of sight, but it is too late. The baby cries out again. I turn back to the blackness and open my eyes.

Down the side of the bed, squeezed tight between the bedstead and the wall, hidden in shadow, is a basket. In the basket is a baby boy. On one fat red leg, he wears one blue shoe.

I look at him and he looks at me, quiet now, waiting. Mine must be the only face he has seen since his mother last gazed down and I swear he is mirroring me, his small lips forming a hopeful 'O'. It turns into a smile as I bend down and put my finger in his tiny, ice-cold hand.

I breathe deeply. The stink has disappeared and I can't smell or taste anything but the adrenaline pumping inside me. Metal on the back of my tongue. The taste of fear. We both know what I'm going to do.

ABOUT THE AUTHORS

NATHALIE ABI-EZZI was born in Beirut and has lived in London since 1973. She has been writing fiction full-time for several years and won the BBC Radio 4 Dotdotdot short story award in 2002. She has just completed her first novel.

PAM AHLUWALIA has a degree from Middlesex University in Writing & Publishing and Media Cultural Studies. She is a founder member of Roti Writers and has performed at festivals and conferences and in The Bollywood Bazaar for Channel Four. Her poetry has been published in an anthology and she is currently working on a novel, from which this is an extract.

MICHAEL CHILOKOA is an up-and-coming Hackney writer who combines a modern style with old influences. He is a beneficiary of Centerprise writing workshops.

STEVE COOK was born and lives in London. He is currently working on a novel and short stories.

BELGIN DURMUSH wrote her first short story eight years ago. She attends Newham Writers' Workshop and enjoys the challenge of writing 'as a means of bringing strange realities to life'.

NICK EDWARDS is thirty years old. He has recently moved from London to Gloucestershire. He has done freelance work for various magazines and *The Independent on Sunday*. This extract is part of his first novel, 'A38 / The Zen Snake'.

ALIX EDWARDS is half-English, half-Italian. She has an MA in Creative Writing from Goldsmiths College and was a winner in the London Short Story Competition in 1994 and the Beyond Words Monologue Competition in 2001. She is currently writing a novel, 'Sweet Pendejo', from which this story is an extract. She plays bass guitar and writes Latin music.

DOUGLAS GORDON spent his formative years in the north west of England, moving to London as a design student. He has since pursued an accidental career as an animator in London and Los Angeles. This will be his first published story and is taken from a recently completed novel, 'Not Lizzie Chalk'.

DONNA GRAY was born in Jamaica. She writes poetry and song lyrics as well as short stories. This story was shortlisted for the Prison Reform Trust annual writing competition and her work has also received Koestler awards.

FATIMA KASSAM is an NUJ-qualified journalist who worked as a research assistant on TV's 'Crimewatch' and as a court reporter. She is now pursuing a fiction-writing career; this is her first published story.

DENESE KEANE is from the Caribbean and enjoys writing 'to express her hopes and dreams'. This story shows how her dream might come true some day.

AYDIN MEHMET ALI was born in Cyprus and came to London to escape war in that country; she has lived most of her life in Hackney. She is an educationalist, intellectual community activist and peace campaigner.

DREDA SAY MITCHELL was born into a Grenadian migrant community in London's East End in 1965. She studied African

History at the School of Oriental and African studies and has an MA in Education Studies from the University of North London. She has worked as a teacher throughout London and is currently an education adviser. This extract is from her first novel.

STEF PIXNER has published a volume of poetry, *Sawdust and White Spirit* (Virago). Her stories have won a Bridport Prize and have been published in *Pretext* (pen and Inc, University of East Anglia) and *The New Writer*. She lives in East London.

KATHARINA RIST was born in 1966 in Germany and has lived in London since 1999, as well as on trains, planes and in other transitory spaces. She has published and broadcast poetry, prose, essays and criticism. She founded the writers' charity Literary Ears in 1998, which involves teaching, editing and translating. This extract is from her novel 'The Halved Man'.

ANITA TADAYON was born in Iran. She came to England to study and now lives in London. This is her first published story.

MONICA TAYLOR was born in East Africa and has lived in Paris and London. She lives with her three daughters and is studying social sciences. She loves travelling and reading.

PAMELA VINCENT was born in the Bronx, New York, and now lives in London where she teaches yoga and gardening, and writes poetry, prose and drama.

JOY WILKINSON is a writer from Lancashire who now lives in London. She writes fiction and plays. Her work has won the Verity Bargate award and been performed at the Soho Theatre and the Old Vic. This extract is from her first novel.

ANOTHER COUNTRY Hélène du Coudray

Ship's officer Charles Wilson arrives in Malta in the early 1920s, leaving his wife and children behind in London. He befriends a Russian émigré family and falls for their governess, the beautiful Maria Ivanovna. The passionate intensity of his feelings propels him into a course of action that promises to end in disaster. First published in 1928, *Another Country* is beautifully written, its prose is fresh and undated, and its themes of exile, love and betrayal are just as relevant today.

H. du Coudray (Hélène Héroys) was born in Kiev in 1906 and spent her childhood in St Petersburg. Just before the Revolution, she escaped first to Finland, then Sweden, before arriving in England at the age of twelve. *Another Country*, written under a pseudonym while she was still a student, won the 1927 (Oxford and Cambridge) University Novel Competition. She wrote three further novels and a biography of Metternich. She died in 1971.

£7.99 ISBN 1 904559 04 2

THE THOUSAND-PETALLED DAISY
Norman Thomas

Injured in a riot while travelling in India, seventeen-year-old Michael Flower is given shelter by a doctor in a white house in an island on a river. There, accompanied by his alter ego (his glove-puppet Mickey-Mack), he meets Om Prakash and his family, a tribe of holy monkeys, and Lila, the beautiful daughter of a diplomat. Unknown to him, the house is also the home of a holy woman. When she grants him an audience, Michael unwittingly incurs the jealousy of her devotee, Hari, and violence unfolds. A storm, a death and a funeral, the delights of first love and the beauty of the Indian landscape are woven into a narrative infused with a distinctive, offbeat humour and a delicate but intensely felt spirituality.

Norman Thomas was born in Wales in 1926. His first novel, *Ask at the Unicorn*, was published in 1963 in the UK and the USA to critical acclaim. He lives in Auroville, South India.

£7.99 ISBN 1 904559 05 0

ON BECOMING A FAIRY GODMOTHER

St. Julians Sara Maitland 28/7/05

'These tales
insistently fill the
vison'—*Times
Literary Supplement*
'Stay curious. Read
Maitland. Take off'—
Spectator
£7.99
ISBN 1 904559 00 X

Fifteen new 'fairy stories' breathe new life into old legends and bring the magic of myth back into modern women's lives. What became of Helen of Troy, of Guinevere and Maid Marion? And what happens to today's mature woman when her children have fled the nest? Here is an encounter with a mermaid, an erotic adventure with a mysterious stranger, the story of a woman who learns to fly and another who transforms herself into a fairy godmother.

IN DENIAL Anne Redmon

'This is intelligent
writing worthy of
a large audience'—
The Times
'Intricate, thoughtful'
—*Times Literary
Supplement*
£7.99
ISBN 1 904559 01 8

In a London prison a serial offender, Gerry Hythe, is gloating over the death of his one-time prison visitor Harriet Washington. He thinks he is in prison once again because of her. Anne Redmon weaves evidence from the past and present of Gerry's life into a chilling mystery. A novel of great intelligence and subtlety, *In Denial* explores themes which are usually written about in black and white, but here are dealt with in all their true complexity.

LEAVING IMPRINTS Henrietta Seredy

'Beautifully written
. . . an unusual and
memorable novel'—
Charles Palliser,
author of
The Quincunx
£7.99
ISBN 1 904559 02 6

'At night when I can't sleep I imagine myself on the island.' But Jessica is alone in a flat by a park. She doesn't want to be there – she doesn't have anywhere else to go. As the story moves between present and past, gradually Jessica reveals the truth behind the compelling relationship that has dominated her life. 'With restrained lyricism, *Leaving Imprints* explores a destructive, passionate relationship between two damaged people. Its quiet intensity does indeed leave imprints. I shall not forget this novel'— Sue Gee, author of *The Hours of the Night*